Inland

Inland

Gerald Murnane

SHEFFIELD – LONDON – NEW YORK

This edition first published in the UK in 2024 by And Other Stories
and originally published by Giramondo in 2013.
Sheffield — London — New York
www.andotherstories.org

Inland published in the UK by Faber & Faber, 1988.
Copyright © 1988, 2013 Gerald Murnane
All rights reserved by and controlled through Giramondo Publishing, Australia.

1 3 5 7 9 8 6 4 2

ISBN: 9781913505820
eBook ISBN: 9781913505837

Typesetter: Tetragon, London; Typefaces: Albertan Pro and Linotype Syntax
(interior) and Stellage (cover); Series Cover Design: Elisa von Randow, Alles Blau
Studio, Brazil, after a concept by And Other Stories; Author Photograph: Ian Hill.

And Other Stories books are printed and bound in the UK on FSC-
certified paper by the CPI Group (UK) Ltd, Croydon. The covers are
of G . F Smith 270gsm Colorplan card — made in the Lake District
at the environmentally friendly James Cropper paper mill — and are
embossed with biodegradable foils from FoilCo, Warrington.

A catalogue record for this book is available from the British Library.

And Other Stories gratefully acknowledge that our work is
supported using public funding by Arts Council England.

Supported using public funding by

**ARTS COUNCIL
ENGLAND**

MIX
Paper | Supporting
responsible forestry
FSC® C171272

I believe that basically you write for two people; yourself to try to make it absolutely perfect…Then you write for who you love whether she can read or write or not and whether she is alive or dead.

ERNEST HEMINGWAY

I am writing in the library of a manor-house, in a village I prefer not to name, near the town of Kunmadaras, in Szolnok County.

These words trailing away behind the point of my pen are words from my native language. Heavy-hearted Magyar, my editor calls it. She may well be right. These words rest lightly on my page, but this heaviness pressing on me is perhaps the weight of all the words I have still not written. And the heaviness pressing on me is what first urged me to write.

Or the heaviness pressing on me could be the weight of all the days I have still not lived. My heaviness will urge me in a little while to get up from this table and to walk to the windows; but the same heaviness will urge me afterwards to sit down again at this table. Then, if I begin to write: *I walked just now to the windows and looked across my estates…* my reader will learn how little I see around me, with this heaviness pressing on me. Of all the wide landscapes around my manor-house, I can never bring to mind any more than the nearest field and the long line of poplar trees on the far side of it.

Is that really all? Sometimes I am aware of more fields behind the first field, and of grasslands behind everything – indistinct grasslands under grey, sagging clouds. And I could repeat a sentence or two from my schooldays: *Szolnok County, on the Great Alföld…*

I have forgotten for the moment what I once read in my schoolbook. But I remember the sweep-arm well in the first field behind the poplar trees.

If you, my reader, could step with me to the windows, you would notice it at once – the long pole pointing at the sky. You would notice the well-pole, but why should I? A long pole points at the sky in every view from every window in this manor-house, and in every view from every manor-house in Szolnok County. Yet again, neither you nor I might see a particular well-pole on the far side of the poplars; one of my overseers was ordered to block the well and to pull down the pole last year – or it may have been another year.

Now, something other than heaviness urges me to leave this table and to walk to the windows. I have to walk to the windows in order to learn whether I remembered, just now, the sight of a certain well, or whether I was dreaming.

But perhaps I could say without leaving this table that I only dreamed of the sight of my well. If you recall, reader, I had not left my table when I began this inquiry. I had only dreamed of myself leaving my table and then returning to my table and then trying to recall what I might have seen through my windows. I dreamed of myself here at my table and then I wondered whether the man I dreamed of – whether that man remembered the sight of a certain well or whether he was dreaming.

I dislike what I have just written. I believe my editor too will dislike it when she reads it. I had not meant to compose that sort of sentence when I began to write. And yet my elaborate sentence has made me forget for a moment the heaviness pressing on me. I will go on with my writing. I will remain at this table. I may not be able to tell you for some time, reader, whether or not a long pole points at the sky in the field behind the poplars. I may even dream of myself stepping to the windows and then returning to this table and then writing about myself having done such things. But if I write any more about the sweep-arm well, I will try for your sake, reader, to distinguish between what I see and what I remember and what I dream of myself seeing or remembering.

My editor lives in the land of America, in the state of South Dakota, in Tripp County, in the town of Ideal. (Not many atlases show this town, but the reader may see the word *Ideal* clearly printed a little east of Dog Ear Creek on page 166 of the *Hammond World Atlas*, published in 1978 by Hammond Incorporated for *Time*.)

My editor lives in America, but she was born where the River Sio, trickling from Lake Balaton, finds an unexpected partner in the River Sarviz from the north. They do not join forces immediately, but wander side by side the whole county through, two or three kilometres apart, winking coquettishly at each other like dreamy lovers. The two streams share one bed, so large, fertile and wide that it might be called a family-size double bed. On either side the gentle slopes and peaceful hills are adorned with colours that would not be out of place on the walls of a serene and cheerful home. This is her part of the world. (Most of the sentences above are copied from *People of the Puszta*, by Gyula Illyes, translated by G. F. Cushing and published by Chatto and Windus in 1971. *People of the Puszta* is not a book of fiction. All the people mentioned in the book were once alive. A few of them may be still alive.)

My editor lives in Ideal, in Tripp County, in South Dakota, but she was born in Tolna County, in Transdanubia, and I like to think that she remembers a little of the district where she spent the first years of her life.

My editor is also my translator. She is fluent in my language and in the American language. She calls herself

Anne Kristaly Gunnarsen. She is married to Gunnar T. Gunnarsen, who is tall and fair-haired and a scientist. He and his wife are both employed in the Calvin O. Dahlberg Institute of Prairie Studies near the town of Ideal. (Calvin Otto Dahlberg was born in Artesian, South Dakota, in 1871 and died at Fond du Lac, Wisconsin, in 1939. He made his fortune from breweries and paper.)

I have never met Gunnar T. Gunnarsen, the scientist of prairies. I have not even met his wife, my editor and translator. But I know that she writes at a desk in a room with books around the walls and a wide window overlooking a prairie.

My editor's prairie is not a true prairie. It is really a wide wasteland owned by the Institute of Prairie Studies. The scientists of the Institute have sown the wasteland with the seeds of every plant that once flourished where the town of Ideal now stands. Each summer, when the plants have grown to their full height, Gunnar T. Gunnarsen and his fellow scientists step gently in among the plants to count them. Unlikely as it seems, the scientists of prairies kneel all day to count and measure on a certain hillside and in a certain hollow and beside a certain pond in the valley of the Dog Ear, on the Great Plain of America. And afterwards the scientists calculate how many more seeds they must sow before the wasteland will have the look and the feel of virgin prairie.

In the meanwhile, Gunnar T. Gunnarsen and his wife

and their thirteen-years-old daughter live in a large house among the experimental plots of the Calvin O. Dahlberg Institute. And sometimes my editor writes to tell me she has just stepped to the windows and she wishes she could describe for me the sight of a wasteland growing into the prairie it should have been always: the sight of her dream-prairie, as she calls it, rising out of the soil around her. My editor writes that she feels herself looking towards the past rather than a vague future. The past is not her own past — not the years of her childhood. She is as far from her childhood as ever. But when she looks out from deep inside the shadows of her room towards the grassland that will soon seem a true prairie, she feels herself about to begin another lifetime in the place where she should have lived always.

But these are only interruptions to the business of her letters. Anne Kristaly Gunnarsen is an intelligent, practical young woman with important affairs in hand. (I will not write here what I privately feel towards the woman who will later read and edit these pages. One day I will write pages that no one will have to edit or translate. I will write about afternoons when I have sat at this table and believed that the last sound I would hear on earth was either the bumping of a window-sash in the summer wind or else the scratching of my pen on paper; that the last sight I would see on earth was either a segment of sky above a row of poplar trees or else the spines of hundreds of books I have never lifted from their shelves. I will write about afternoons when I might have been smothered under a heaviness if I had not found on my table a few pages like these around me now: pages from the land of America, where people write freely to one another and are never alone.)

My editor has turned into Magyar for me the names of plants that she sees from her window. She urges me to write the names of her admired plants and to recite them aloud. She assures me I will feel a rare pleasure as I name in my own language the grasses and shrubs from her dream-prairie in America. She wants me, so she says, to see here in Szolnok County the nodding of tiny blue and scarlet flowers; to hear on my own plains the rattling of strange grass-stems in the wind. Sometimes my editor even urges me to turn my own fields and pastures into a dream-grassland, or to establish an Institute of Great Alfold Studies on some patch of wasteland among the outlying streets of Kunmadaras.

I hardly feel my heaviness when Anne Kristaly Gunnarsen writes so earnestly to me. I cannot do all that she urges me to do. But sometimes I write the names of plants from her dream-prairie. And sometimes I recite the names – not with pleasure exactly but with a queer mixture of feelings.

Here are some of the names for you to recite, reader. But perhaps you will hear, as you recite, only sounds of heavy-hearted Magyar.

Little bluestem; ironweed; fleabane; boneset; wolfberry; chokeberry.

(All the names of plants in the paragraph above can be found in *The Life of Prairies and Plains* by Durward L. Allen, published in 1967 by McGraw-Hill Book Company in co-operation with The World Book Encyclopedia.)

Anne Kristaly Gunnarsen translates much more than names of grasses and shrubs. She is director of the Bureau for the Exchange of Data on Grasslands and Prairies. The Bureau is a department within the Institute of Prairie Studies.

When I first heard of the Bureau, I dreamed of a large American building crowded with filing cabinets and desks and with clerks wearing green eyeshades. But Anne Kristaly Gunnarsen speaks lightly of the Bureau. She tells me it is literally a desk – the same desk from which she writes to me. And she diminishes the Bureau by naming it from the initial letters of its title.

Sometimes Anne Kristaly Gunnarsen describes herself sitting at her desk and thinking of the grasslands of the world. At every hour of the day, in one country or another, a man looks up from peering at plants with names such as ironweed or wolfberry. The man is the only person inside the circle of the horizon. He stares across the veldt or the steppes or the pampas and prepares to think of himself as quite alone. But he cannot think of himself and the grass around his knees and the clouds over his head and nothing more. He thinks of himself talking or writing to a young woman. He thinks of himself telling the young woman that he thinks of her whenever he finds himself alone in grasslands. He thinks of himself telling the young woman that he thinks of her telling him she thinks of a man such as himself whenever she sits at her desk and thinks of the grasslands of the world.

According to my editor, all the level and grassy places of the world are marked on maps and described on sheaves of paper in the Bureau for the Exchange of Data on Grasslands and Prairies. Every day the director of the Bureau sits at her desk and reads about the plains of the world. The men on their veldts and steppes and prairies are thinking about Anne Kristaly Gunnarsen in the place that she calls BEDGAP.

Every night in summer Anne Kristaly Gunnarsen leaves the windows of her bedroom open wide. The last sound that my editor hears before she falls asleep is either the clashing of small seed-pods in the night breeze or else the soft thud and the faint metallic echo of a beetle or a moth against the window-screen.

Anne Kristaly Gunnarsen's dream-prairie begins at her window. Instead of lawns and gardens around their houses, the prairie-scientists of Ideal let the wild kinds of grass grow freely. If Anne Kristaly opens her eyes in the night, she sees between herself and the moon and stars blade-shapes and spear-shapes and helmet-shapes, or sometimes the shapes of feathers or bells or bonnets.

My editor has never told me, and I will never ask, but I believe she sleeps alone in her room. All night she is only wakened, I believe, by scents. Every day on her dream-prairie countless flowers almost too small to see burst out at the ends of grasses. Each flower spills particles and droplets in the air. Every night the air of Ideal has the taste of the inner parts of flowers, and all night in her room my editor takes this rich air into her throat.

You must have noticed, reader, that I cannot write easily about the scents of things. I was born with a strange deformity: my nose has no power of smelling.

The wind in my face might have come to me straight from the hills and valleys of wet dung where the female farm-servants have heaped the scrapings from my cattle-barns. Or the wind comes from the roses on the many archways over the winding paths to my ornamental lake. But I get from the wind no hint of dung or roses. I only feel the rush or the drift of the air, and all I think of is the width of land that the air has crossed before it reaches me.

If I were to write to my editor that I have taken pleasure from scents on the Great Alfold, I would be deceiving her. But I pretend to understand her when she writes that her room has been sweetened all night by some scent from her dream-prairie.

The official organ of the Calvin O. Dahlberg Institute of

Prairie Studies is called *Hinterland*. The first number of *Hinterland* was expected to appear long before now. Anne Kristaly Gunnarsen tells me the issue has been delayed because the position of editor has not yet been filled and because scientists and writers have disagreed about the purpose of the official organ of the Institute.

I do not know who finally controls the Institute of Prairie Studies. I used to believe that my editor, with all those grasslands at her windows and all those books on her shelves, would have had few people above her. But sometimes she writes of having to impress certain men and of having to court and flatter them because she has set her heart on being editor of *Hinterland*.

For the time being, Anne Kristaly Gunnarsen is free to solicit items for publication. I believe her husband procures from among his fellow scientists part of what she requires. And every day, from some distant state of America, a student of prairies or a writer she has never met sends a bulky parcel of typescript pages and surprising photographs, hoping to win her favour.

Days and nights have passed since I began to write on these pages. You need not ask, reader, what might have happened in this house or on my estates or anywhere in Szolnok County while I have been at my writing. I have a wife who also lives in this house, along with my youngest daughter. I have servants and animals and farmhands and fields and pastures. But these have always seemed not quite real to me.

I have spent much of my life watching white or grey clouds drifting over my flat lands while I dreamed of being known in some place of more consequence than Szolnok County. Another sort of man – my father who died young or my grandfather who founded this library – might have dreamed of a book with his name on its spine or on some of its pages. But the sight of these books around me only adds to my heaviness. Who could want his name or his story buried in a book? Seasons and whole years pass while this room of books remains deserted – except for myself, and a young female servant who comes quietly each week and scatters the dust on the locked glass doors in front of the shelves.

No one unlocks the glass doors in front of my books, but sometimes I stand in front of the glass and I wonder what lies behind all the dull-coloured spines and covers. Sometimes, in the late afternoon, I see in one of the glass doors an image of the windows behind me. I see an image of clouds drifting across the sky, and I think of the white or grey pages of books drifting across the space behind covers and spines. Clouds drift through the sky, and the pages of books drift through the libraries of manor-houses. Clouds and pages drift across the Great Alfold and away towards the skies and the libraries of other countries. And other clouds and other pages drift over the plains of the world towards the skies and the libraries of Szolnok County.

But these pages lie safely on my table. These are not

the drifting pages of books. My pages will never drift across the skies in the libraries of this country or any other country. I am not writing on clouds. I am not writing on pages of books. I am writing to my editor. I am writing to a living woman.

I have been searching among the pages on this table for the letters from Anne Kristaly Gunnarsen to me. I would like to read again today the letter from my editor begging me to send her some of these pages.

Write to me, my editor wrote to me. *Send me your paragraphs, your pages, your stories of the Great Alfold. Write what may well decide my future in the Calvin O. Dahlberg Institute.*

On many days, before I began this writing, I kept to my library and watched the clouds passing and thought of my editor's latest letter to me. I wanted to prolong the pleasure of having a young woman in America so anxious to read my pages.

I supposed the contest for the position of editor of *Hinterland* had grown more fierce. Some powerful man within the Institute of Prairie Studies had stepped up to the desk of Anne Kristaly Gunnarsen and had stood between my editor and the window. The man had warned Anne Kristaly Gunnarsen that people looking into *Hinterland* in time to come would be looking for pages sent by men from prairies and plains to the young women who were their editors and translators.

Then, so I supposed, the powerful man from the Institute of Prairie Studies had walked to the window and had stared out across the gentle valleys where boneset and little bluestem grow. If any man within the Institute of Prairie Studies could ever have dreamed of a man such as myself here in Szolnok County on the Great Alfold, then the man staring out through the windows that Anne Kristaly Gunnarsen stared through so often would have dreamed of me at that moment.

But I can only suppose the man at the window would have said to Anne Kristaly Gunnarsen that he was thinking just then of the pages of *Hinterland*. He was thinking of himself looking at the pages of *Hinterland* and thinking of grasslands far away from America and on those grasslands manor-houses and in each of those manor-houses a man sitting alone at a table in a library with a window-sash that bumps sometimes faintly in the wind.

Afterwards the man who had warned Anne Kristaly Gunnarsen stepped into the rooms of one after another of her rivals and warned them in the same way. Then the man I have only dreamed of went back to his own room high up in the Institute of Prairie Studies and walked to his window and stared at the same prairie that Anne Kristaly Gunnarsen stared at so often, except that he could see from his high window a little more of grassland than she could see and perhaps a line of trees in the distance.

Now all three of us keep to our rooms. The man in the Calvin O. Dahlberg Institute stares out from his window and waits for Anne Kristaly Gunnarsen to come to him with a stack of pages in her arms. Anne Kristaly Gunnarsen herself stares out at the place that she calls her dream-prairie. She thinks of a red roof among green treetops; of the white gleam of sunlight on a lake; of pathways winding under arches of roses and past beds of canna and agapanthus. And she waits for my pages to come to her.

I myself do just as I have already written. I sit at this table and sometimes I write a little, or I dream of myself writing.

I have been writing about myself dreaming about the Calvin O. Dahlberg Institute of Prairie Studies when I should have been writing about my editor begging me to write to her.

On many days before I began writing on these pages, I thought I would make my editor pay a price for my pages. I would compel her to answer questions that I had wanted for many years to ask. I would ask her about the year when she turned from a child into a young woman. I would ask her about the young man who first unfastened her clothing in the district where the Sio and the Sarviz flow side by side. I would ask her what she remembered of that young man when the breeze at night drifted in from her dream-prairie.

When Anne Kristaly Gunnarsen signs a letter, her name reaches far out towards the centre of the page. If I look at her name for long enough, all her ens and esses turn into grass-stems and all the grass-stems lean as though a wind is blowing over them. If I stare at a page from Anne Kristaly Gunnarsen I can see words turning into grass – long, silken Magyar grass that would touch my thighs if I walked among it; short and brittle American grass that I could trample; and down below the tangle of stems, boneset or chokeberry or tiny reds and blues with no names in her language or mine.

Today when I remember the writing of the person who begged me to write, I see the penstrokes of someone who dreams hardly ever of grasslands.

I think of Gunnar T. Gunnarsen, scientist of prairies. I think of the stern Swede with his cold skin clamped every night against my warm and nervous editor. He believes his wife has kept hidden for all these years some secret of Transdanubia where she was born. He has counted the grass-stems and the flowering bushes on the dream-prairie of Anne Kristaly Gunnarsen, but he suspects that his wife once strolled with me between the Sio and the Sarviz and he wants to know what secrets Anne Kristaly shares with me that she will not share with her Swede husband.

And now the scientist of prairies has signed his wife's name beneath a letter asking me to send her some pages from the Great Alfold. He pretends to be my editor and translator so that I will write to him about a stream trickling among stones, dragonflies poised above the reeds, storm-clouds gathering behind the poplar trees, a young woman beside me in the grass...But if I write about such things, no more letters will come to me from America. Gunnar T. Gunnarsen will sign my name on a letter to Anne Kristaly Gunnarsen. The letter will tell my editor that I have died and been buried in the district where I was born; that I lie under the grass on the Great Alfold and under the drifting clouds.

Now, having written this, I see that the husband of Anne Kristaly has always wanted me dead. I see him crouched among the wolfberry on the dream-prairie of Anne Kristaly and hating me because I see him and he cannot see me.

My editor will read the letter calmly, but afterwards she will sit at her desk all afternoon writing a notice to appear in the rear pages of *Hinterland*, among reviews of books about childhoods spent hundreds of miles from sea-coasts, advertisements for holidays to be spent in houses with hundreds of windows overlooking level countryside, requests for companions male or female for expeditions to far corners of America, requests for pen-friends female only from remote districts plains preferred or gentle hills definitely no mountains or sea-coasts...

I have spent a whole afternoon writing the notice that Anne Kristaly Gunnarsen will display at the rear of her publication.

I have tried to insert something of myself into the passage below.

OBITUARY NOTICE

There died quietly some little time ago, at his family seat in Szolnok County on the Great Alfold, a gentleman who preserved during a lifetime spent almost wholly in the seclusion of his ancestral library, or in solitary walks though the extensive park and grounds laid out by his grandfather, a secret so burdensome that no writer of fiction would dare implant it in the heart of any one of his characters for fear of ridicule.

The gentleman had a particular enthusiasm for the literature and the flora of other nations. His servants speak admiringly of his standing for long periods before the shelves of his library or among the massed displays of his exotic blooms. His love of books one can readily understand as the mental voyaging of a man confined for private reasons behind the walls of his manorial park. As for his botanising, the gentleman was often heard to aver that he loved his plants for what he chose to call their constancy.

Skies, landscapes, even the familiar gables and turrets that we glimpse at the end of each journey homewards, and not least the features and the gestures of our dear ones – all these so change or are changed in time that none of us can say what is the true appearance of the person or the thing that he loves. Yet unfailingly each year, on some humble bush or clump which first we peered at as timid or lonely children, the petals unfold of the exact hue and shape, of the very same number, and at the precise points around the flower-rim as of old, and we recognise that something at least of all we have loved has kept faith with us.

These sentiments from a famous foreign writer, whose works in translation must surely have graced the shelves of the gentleman's library, might well have been written by the gentleman himself in order to explain his retiring often to the depths of his garden. Why he strove thus to erect before his eyes an image of his earlier life we may hesitate to ask. But something of his state of mind on many an afternoon among his quiet avenues we may surmise from the report of a witness. This was a young woman, a farm-servant and a member of a family which later found its way to America. Even at the time of the gentleman's death, the woman could describe vividly a sight that had met her eyes many years earlier. In her own unadorned words:

In those days one of my habitual routes took me past a corner of the great park where the brick wall gave way for a considerable distance to upright spikes of metal. On the afternoon in question my eye was taken by an area of unusually vivid colour a little distance beyond the fence. I pressed my face against the upright metal. (It was unexpectedly warm, and I observed at the time that either the afternoon sun had much more strength than I had supposed or the long poles retained for a surprising length of time the heat of noonday.) Then, on looking towards the remarkable colour, I saw that it came from a dense cluster of the blooms whose name in my mother tongue is tiger-lily.

The flowers seemed at first so closely massed that I might have been observing one fabric formed from the stitching together of a hundred petals. And at first, the intense glow that had attracted me seemed to come from the flowers all having intercepted, for that little space of time, the level rays of the almost-sunken sun.

But I soon observed that although the patchwork of petals was a uniform lily-colour, still one small area contrasted oddly with its surroundings. The small area had none of the tiny brown spots and blotches that seem on tiger-lilies so like freckles on golden skin. The unfreckled patch seemed odd because it was the one part of the fabric that did not resemble skin. Yet it was itself skin: the face of a man clean-shaven and with hair receding from his forehead and eyes downcast.

Although my own family were farm-servants, I was not quite ignorant of the ways of the gentry. My mother in her youth had had some dealings with the family whose head now showed his head to me in a bed of lilies. I knew that the polite course for me was to betray no surprise or concern at having come upon the owner of our lands engaged in some private ritual in a natural setting. No doubt I glanced upwards at the fierce pointed ends of the fence-poles barring the way to my master's domain, and shuddered at the image of impalement that came to me. Yet I sensed that my master was aware of my presence without being disposed just then to drive me away. I had not actually seen his eyes on me, but I was somehow convinced that he had been watching me – and not just on that afternoon but perhaps for days past, whenever I had come that way. I therefore fixed my gaze on a pale and somewhat furrowed pink that I took to be the lowered lid over one of my master's eyeballs, and I waited to hear what he wanted from me.

I had not been gazing for long at my master when the sun fell suddenly below the western horizon, whereupon I noticed that although the gold and the freckle-brown were fading rapidly from the petals of the lilies, on the face at their centre a mild flush or glow persisted. I resolved there and then to occupy myself for as long as my master was *still preparing himself to address me by speculating on the condition of his heart in whose face such a light...*

I need not go on with this writing. Anne Kristaly Gunnarsen would be able to bring it to a fitting end. She would write that the man kept his face to the horizon until the last colour was gone from the sky and the long pole above the well in the middle distance had quite disappeared. She would write what the man might have said at last to the young woman and what the young woman might have answered. She would know how to fill with words the deep rectangle edged with black below the photograph of my family graveyard in some out-of-the-way page of *Hinterland*.

My editor has never seen a photograph of me. I have not wanted to remind her of the difference between her age and mine. But I am preparing to send her a picture of my family graveyard. I will send the picture not because of the tombstones and the names engraved on them but because I understand that my editor sometimes finds in graveyards a few stems of a grass or a small flowering plant that once flourished where farms and villages and cities now stand. In certain graveyards in America a patch of unmown grass between two tombstones may be the only place in all the county where the same plants grow, and in the same numbers, as grew in that place long before my editor and I were born.

Anne Kristaly Gunnarsen sometimes visits these graveyards. No heaviness presses on her while she walks between the stones. When she kneels with her face close to the soil, she sees what may well be virgin prairie. If she thinks of herself dying she is not afraid. Even if she dies, she thinks, some of the men who once wrote to her will go on writing.

I am thinking today of the pages of *Hinterland* in all the years when my editor will think of me as dead. I am prepared to have my editor think of me as dead, but I wonder what will become of all the pages I was going to send to her. Anne Kristaly Gunnarsen once wrote that she would lay my pages under the eyes of men and women who have never seen, nor will ever see, the Great Alfold, but who want to breathe with ecstasy, through the curtain of the falling rain, the scent of invisible yet enduring flowers with mournful-sounding Magyar names.

I am ready to go on writing although my editor believes I am dead. But if I send my pages in a parcel to America, the leader of a gang of scientists will seize my pages before they reach the desk of my editor.

The Swede scientist has always hated me. He strides out from among the folds of my editor's dream-prairie and towards the staircase of grey marble, then up the staircase and between the columns of white marble and under the carved gold letters, CALVIN O. DAHLBERG

INSTITUTE OF PRAIRIE STUDIES, then in through the tall doors of black glass. He goes on striding over carpet geranium-red and between green blades of potted palms. He steps into the elevator-cage. The servant-girl, in livery green or brown with sky-blue trim, looks shyly up at the eyes of ice-blue. She presses a button brass or bronze and the cage is hauled by cables upwards. The scientist and the servant-girl stand far apart in the cage, but his body and her body sway and shudder in sympathy past floor after floor of geranium-red, and windows after windows with sights of wider and wider land.

My enemy takes long strides across the topmost of all the layers of geranium-red. The windows at his back show prairies true and false on the Great Plain of America, and in the farthest distance a building white with a golden dome in the city of Lincoln in the state of Nebraska. In the chandelier above him, the prisms and cylinders of glass are clustered like the skyscrapers on the island of Manhattan. My enemy strides towards a door with HINTERLAND stamped in gold leaf on a pane of frosted glass.

A boy-man in livery dark-grey with gold trim and a hat strangely flattened appears from around a corner and takes rapid goose-steps towards the same door that my enemy approaches. The boy-man holds his right hand near his right ear, with palm upward and fingers splayed. The splayed fingers support a silver salver. On the salver is a parcel of brown paper with many-coloured postage-stamps in rows like military decorations.

The boy-man is first to the door by a margin of five paces. He reaches his left hand towards a button in a circular recess beside the door. Gunnar T. Gunnarsen arrives at the door. He grips the boy-man's left wrist in his brown right hand and whispers an instruction.

The boy-man makes no move to obey the instruction. The tall Swede moves his brown left hand also to the left wrist of the boy-man and then grips the frail wrist and twists his own hands in opposite directions around the wrist. The Swede scientist gives the boy-man what American children call a Chinese burn.

The boy-man bends his body violently backwards. The silver salver and the decorated parcel fall to the carpeted floor. Neither bounces; each falls flat. The geranium-red is deep and yielding.

The Swede releases the boy-man and then stoops. He picks up the parcel and then strides off around a corner and down a corridor where the carpet is ankle-deep and flecked with green-grey.

The door marked HINTERLAND is opened quietly from within. The boy-man turns to face the doorway. The person inside the room stands just beyond the doorway so that I see only the tips of a pair of ladies' shoes. Higher up I see a female hand reaching out towards the boy-man's hand in a gesture offering comfort.

I strain to see the female who offers comfort. I view the scene from several vantage-points. I see the corner of an enormous desk in the room beyond the open door. I see black or violet lettering on yellow or lilac spines of books on shelves against a wall. I see heaps of grey clouds in the sky beyond the window beyond the door, and below the grey clouds the orange-gold of a plain covered with ripened wheat, and deep beneath the plain the words: *Gray and Gold; John Rogers Cox; Cleveland Museum of Art.* From between the grey clouds a shaft of sunlight picks out the pointed bell-tower of a small church of white timber far away to the east, in the valley of the Merrimack in Middlesex County; another shaft of sunlight reaches down through the window of the room labelled HINTERLAND and touches the face of the boy-man, which is thick with freckles, and picks out a single teardrop on his cheek. The teardrop magnifies a particular red-brown freckle. The female hand begins to stroke the clay-coloured hair standing stiffly out from under the boy-man's flattened hat. The hand is withdrawn and then returns to view with a small white handkerchief in its grasp. On a corner of the handkerchief is embroidered a spray of the leaves and fruit of the tree whose name in my language is *mulberry*. The hand with the handkerchief wipes away the tear from the cheek, and then every tear from the eyes. The bell in the church begins to ring.

Now I stand as well in that place. My feet are deep in red and the red is flecked with green-grey. My feet are heavy to lift, and I wonder why the people around me are stepping so lightly.

I walk to a low table and a group of chairs five paces from my editor's door. I sit in a chair that tilts me far backwards, and I lower my eyes.

I look up, and I see that the door labelled HINTERLAND has been closed. Around me at the low table, seated men and women hold outspread covers of illustrated magazines in front of their faces. On the covers of the magazines, shafts of yellow light fall on white churches, on trees with orange or red leaves beside dark-green streams trickling, and on boy-men walking towards the streams. The boy-men have fishing-rods on their shoulders and twigs or grass-stems between their front teeth. A shaft of sunlight touches the face of one of the boy-men and picks out teardrops. A little bell rings monotonously. I look far into the pictures around me for some other place that some of the boy-men might be walking towards. But all the boy-men, and even the boy-man with the tears on his face, are walking towards streams in America.

I climb out of my chair and I look among the magazines on the low table. Each name on a magazine is in the American language. On the covers of some magazines are pictures of indistinct grasslands under grey clouds, but none of the names on those covers is *Hinterland*.

The boy-man in livery dark-grey with gold trim appears from around a corner. On his silver salver he carries a bottle of whisky and drinking glasses and a jar with silver machinery on top. He pushes open the door marked HINTERLAND and walks in without knocking and leaves the door open behind him. I see clearly the desk and the person sitting behind it. The person is a man with an American bow-tie of white spots on black; he is a stranger to me.

The boy-man places the silver salver on the desk. The man with the spotted bow-tie pours whisky for himself and for one other person out of my view. Then the man with the bow-tie sets the machinery working on the jar, and frothing water spurts into the glass that will go to the person out of my view. The boy-man turns to leave the room, but the man with the bow-tie signals to him and pours him a small measure of the whisky. The boy-man smiles at last.

I look again at the table in front of me. I want to look once more at the picture of the boy-man with the tears on his face. The picture is not where I last saw it. I look at the covers of magazines in front of the faces of people around the table. One face is hidden behind swamps, with flocks of birds circling overhead, in Buenos Aires County far away but not so long ago. The face of a young female is hidden behind the plains of Melbourne County, where spiked and thorny bushes grow, and stones and boulders lie. One of the persons with faces hidden behind flat land is a young woman with silk stockings. I suspect from the shape of the legs and from other signs that this is the woman I used to call my editor when I lived on the Great Alfold.

In front of the face of the woman with the silk stockings is a view of a landscape so level and so vast that it can only lie in the steppes of Central Asia. And now I know that this woman is my editor. This woman with her legs in silk and her face behind a desert of grass is Anne Kristaly Gunnarsen, and she is about to look at me after all these years. She has hidden herself here with her supporters in order to win back the room and the desk and the books on the shelves that should be hers, and she is about to beg me to help her.

Yet I do not want the woman to look at me. She will look into my face and I will have to speak to her. I will have to explain to her what I meant by all those pages that I covered with my writing when I was a man in the library of a manor-house and she was a young woman looking out at her dream-prairie near the town of Ideal. All this is too much to explain.

I reach towards the table for a page to put in front of my own face. The young female lowers from in front of her face the view of thorn-bushes and grass and stones on the plains of Melbourne County. She is hardly more than a child. She tosses the magazine onto the table. I pick up the magazine from where it has fallen. I am about to hide my own face.

But just now, across the table and on the other side of the heap of pages with views of grasslands in many countries, the landscape in the steppes of Central Asia is lifted away and I see the face behind it.

The face is only one of many faces such as I have seen in my lifetime, here in Szolnok County. It could hardly be the face of the woman I have called my editor for so long.

My own face, from long habit, has remained stern, unblinking. Neither the young woman nor the child will ever know that I was mistaken about her.

Elsewhere in a corridor of the building, I lift my feet with effort through flecks of green-grey in geranium-red. I look down and I see the green-grey stirring like dust and then settling again into the red. I understand that powerful people in this building and rivals for the position of editor of *Hinterland* have torn open in this corridor all the parcels of pages addressed to their enemies and rivals. They have torn open the parcels and unfastened from the pages the leaves and the grass-stems pressed and dried and the grass-flowers mounted as in life. They have ground into dust between their fingers the sword-shape and the feather-shape and every bell-shape with its tongue-shape dangling inside. And then they have let the dust drift down from their fingers to settle among tufts and strands geranium-red.

I have found bell-shapes sometimes growing by hundreds in my family graveyard. I have pressed and dried a handful of the bell-shapes between blank pages of writing-paper under a stack of the largest books from my shelves. I had hoped to send a page of the pressed leaves and flowers to Anne Kristaly Gunnarsen. I know of no name for the bell-shapes in my language, but I thought my editor would surmise from the look of the dried things on the page how the bell-shapes had swung in the wind when the sap was in them. I thought she would remember having seen the bell-shapes during her childhood between the Sio and the Sarviz. I thought she might have told me the name she used as a child for the bell-shapes, and where she had seen them, and how she had shaken them on their stalks.

Now in these corridors I see the green-grey dust of all the plants that men from grasslands have sent to the women they call their editors. If my nose could be of any use to me, I would kneel in these corridors and press my face into the red. I would try to learn what kinds of leaves and flowers other men once hoped to send to their editors. I would like to write much more about the skyscraper of glass and marble on the Great Plain of America. I remember that I saw from one of the windows of the skyscraper two or three young women far away, by a fish pond with floating leaves and flowers on a lawn in front of the white building with the golden dome in Lincoln, in Lancaster County, in the state of Nebraska.

Even from so far away, I could see a book in the hands of one of the young women. And I understood that the young woman wanted to show me something on one of the pages of the book. I have never looked into any of the books in my own library, but the young woman by the fish pond wanted me to meet her in Lancaster County and to look at something she had found in a book.

From where I stood, high up in the Calvin O. Dahlberg

Institute, all the land between Ideal, South Dakota, and Lancaster County, Nebraska, was a lawn with ornamental ponds and streams. Instead of villages or towns I saw patches of orange-gold or red-brown like the pattern of flower-beds in the garden that I see from the windows of my library. I waited for the young woman with the book in her hand to begin to walk towards me from beside the fish pond. I waited to watch her crossing the wide lawn among the flower-beds and shrubs and coming slowly nearer the district of Ideal.

Then I remembered where I was: where I have always been. And I thought of the young woman approaching Ideal and finding herself in grass with the look and the feel of virgin prairie. The young woman looks up at the rows of glass panes on the building of the Institute of Prairie Studies. She sees the shapes of men and women behind the greyish glass and she supposes that one of those shapes is myself. She does not know that I am far away in my library in Szolnok County.

I would like to write more about the skyscraper of marble and glass on the Great Plain of America, but that sort of writing is by no means easy. I have written that sort of writing only since I first thought of my editor as thinking of me as dead.

It is not easy to think of myself as a man who is thought of as dead. I might as easily think of myself as dead. And perhaps this is what some writers do before they begin to write. They think of themselves as dead. Or they think of themselves as thought of as dead.

I have always understood that the people whose names are on the pages of my books are all dead. Some of those people were once alive but now they are dead. Others of those people have never been alive; they have always been dead.

Today I am thinking of the people whose names are on the covers of books: the same people who wrote the pages inside the books. I have always supposed that all of those people are dead. But I used to suppose that the people first wrote the pages of the books and then died. They wrote their books and then they died. Today I believe that the people who wrote the pages of the books may have died before they wrote. They died, or they thought of themselves as having died, or they thought of themselves as thought of as dead – and then they wrote.

On a certain day in a certain year a writer of books arrived at the front door of my manor-house. Why did the writer of books visit me of all men? When I asked the writer that question he told me politely that all my questions would be answered when I read the book that he was writing. The book would be about people who were alive and had not died, and about grasslands.

On a certain afternoon when more clouds than usual were drifting over my estates, a writer of books stepped into this library and told me his name. If ever I had seen the name on the spine or the cover of a book, I might have remembered the name today. I only remember, however, that the writer of books was born in Transdanubia, in Tolna County. And perhaps you ought to conclude from this, reader, that something in the soil of that county urges men and women to become writers or readers of books, or to die or to read about people who are dead.

If the writer of books had already died before he called at my manor-house, then the man who stepped into this library was a ghost. As a ghost he was able to stand at any window in any manor-house on the Great Alfold, but he stood for a while at the window where I sometimes stand, and he stared at the row of poplar trees and the same almost-empty fields that I sometimes stare at.

If the writer of books was a ghost, did he see the same view that I see from my window? I believe the writer of books saw the ghosts of things from my window. He saw things that I might have seen long ago but cannot see today. He saw the arm of a well, perhaps, that I no longer see. He saw men and women, perhaps, who no longer live on my estates.

I told my guest, the writer of books, that my library and my estates were his. But the writer of books wanted only to look out through one after another of my windows and then to walk around the boundaries of my park.

I walked with the writer of books to the place where the brick wall gives way to the iron spikes. The writer looked back in the direction of my manor-house. He stared at the high fence around the tennis courts. The fence is overgrown by an ornamental vine, and the writer of books saw the vine when its leaves were red – so red that I preferred not to look at them.

The writer of books spoke to me. Some of what he said was in his and my native language, but sometimes he seemed to be speaking in the language of ghosts, which is even more heavy-hearted. He said he would write in a book that a redness had overhung my manor-house when he called on me. But he said also that he would write also about the whiteness that would have been seen from my library window on a morning in winter. And I understood him to say also that he would write also that a greenness would have met the eye of anyone who walked out onto my estates and looked down into a well.

(Whitney Smith, Executive Director of the Flag Research Center, Winchester, Massachusetts, and author of *Flags Through the Ages and Across the World*, McGraw-Hill (UK), Maidenhead, 1975, writes that the red comes from the flag of Arpad in the ninth century, which was all red; the white comes from Saint Stephen, who introduced a white cross into the national coat-of-arms in the eleventh century; the green is the green of the low hills from which the cross was shown as rising.)

Late in the afternoon the writer of books saw the sky filling with clouds and said he would spend the night in my manor-house.

The writer and I dined alone together and afterwards retired to the library and sat at the fireside. Some people have called me a dull man, but I knew that the writer of books was waiting to question me as soon as the wine had made me talkative. Before he could ask his questions, I challenged him to a game: I would pretend to be a writer of books and he would pretend to be a man who looked out from the windows of his library in a manor-house in Szolnok County.

The writer of books nodded absently, and I supposed he had agreed to take part in my game. I got pen and paper from my table and took brief notes, as though I was in fact a writer of books who would write one day about himself and the man in the library of the manor-house.

The firelight glimmered in the mellow gold of the wine and the ornate gilt lettering on the sombre volumes behind the glass of the bookcase. The wind thumped and cried eerily at the windows like the ghosts of lost children beating their fists on the panes and pleading to be taken in. An occasional gust was heard in the chimney, causing the flames in the grate to bend violently sideways. Sipping contentedly from their glasses, the two men stared into the flames and spoke in quiet tones.

'One thing I've always been a little curious about,' said the writer, tapping his glass idly with a fingernail and trying to appear somewhat bored by his subject. 'You chaps in your manor-houses out here on the Great Alfold…do you handle your young heifers when they come of age? pinch their flanks? squeeze their pointed udders? stretch their little breeding-parts for them?' He paused...'And how do the young heifers take to this? Do they let fly with their dainty hoofs? Do they bellow for their mothers?'

(Some people have called me a dull man, but I had known all along why the writer of books had visited my manor-house.)

The man from Szolnok County eyed his questioner shrewdly over the rim of his glass. 'You'll have your answer just as soon as I learn whether you writers of books in Transdanubia tamper with your yearling sows before you send them to the boar!'

The man from Szolnok County had expected the writer of books to fling his head back at this and to laugh, which would have been the signal for the glasses to be refilled and the two men of the world to clap one another about the shoulders and embark on a frank exchange of reminiscences.

'Ah, yes!' the man from Szolnok County had expected the writer of books to say with a knowing smile. 'Ah, yes! Our chubby yearling sows! They have to be scrubbed first, most of them. We tame them with a glass or two of the very wine you have in your hand. We tame them first and then we stand by to see them scrubbed. Or we scrub them with our own hands if we dare; we scrub them until their hams are red and glowing. Then we unwrap our own meat, our flitches of well-cured bacon, and we and the chubby young sows pig it together. And they thank us afterwards, most of the little pink sows; they thank us with tears in their eyes for having taught them how to enjoy a piece of good old well-cured Transdanubian bacon.'

If the writer of books had uttered these words, smiling quietly and moistening his lips with his tongue from time to time, then the man from Szolnok County would have answered: 'You writers of books from across the river are welcome to your plump young sows, but this is cattle country here on the Great Alfold. Our heifers are not bred for wallowing in bathtubs or for having their haunches shined with soap. The legs of our heifers are long and their shanks are lean, and the frisky creatures lead us a merry chase before we throw them. But we always catch them and throw them in the end. We throw them down, and they wave their long white legs in the air, and then we prod the heifers, and they lie still for a little while. Yet our young cattle are full of spirit, and not the least of our pleasures is to see them toss their pretty heads and kick up their heels at us when we turn them loose afterwards on our grasslands.'

If both the writer of books from Tolna County and the man from the library in Szolnok County had gone thus far in exchanging confidences, then perhaps one or the other would have asked the question whether from among all his droves of sows or heifers a man might remember a particular young female for long after he had sent her back to his sties or his pastures.

Who knows into what deep places their talk might have led the writer of books and the man from the manor-house? But, in fact, neither man would talk openly of heifers or young sows. The writer of books talked about the pages of books, and the man from the library of the manor-house talked about the grasslands of America. The writer of books talked about a young woman who was dead, and the man from the library talked about a woman who was alive and well and living on the Great Plain of America and who sometimes wrote to him.

After a lengthy silence, during which both men eyed each other searchingly, the man from Szolnok County declared that he had been preparing for some time to write on a few pages and to send the pages to the young woman in America, but he was afraid that if he wrote on too many pages someone in America might bind the pages into a book with his name on it, after which the people of America might well suppose he was dead.

At this, the writer of books leapt suddenly to his feet, drained his glass with a flourish, and strode purposefully to the glass door of a bookcase on a shadowy wall. Gesturing passionately towards the hundreds of volumes, he announced:

'You are dreaming of yourself writing in the library of a manor-house, in Szolnok County, but while you were dreaming at your table I was writing on pages of books.

'You are dreaming of yourself writing to a young woman in America, but in all the years while I was writing, no young woman wrote to me from America or from any other country.

'I am a writer of books. I have died. I never saw, nor ever could have seen, the land of America, but I wanted to breathe with ecstasy, through the curtain of the falling rain, the scent of invisible yet enduring dream-prairies.

'I am a writer of books. I am a ghost. While I was writing I died and became a ghost. While I was writing I saw ghosts of hundreds of books that I have never seen, nor will ever see, in libraries where ghosts of men that I have never seen, nor will ever see, dreamed of writing to young women in America. I saw ghosts of my own books in ghosts of libraries where no one comes to unlock the glass doors of bookcases. I saw ghosts of men staring sometimes at ghosts of glass panes. I saw ghosts of images of clouds drifting through the ghost of an image of sky behind ghosts of covers and spines of ghosts of books. I saw ghosts of images of pages white or grey drifting through the same ghost of an image of sky. And I went on writing so that ghosts of images of pages of mine would drift over ghosts of plains in a ghost of a world towards ghosts of images of skies in libraries of ghosts of the ghosts of books.'

The writer of books took up my challenge. He pretended to be the man from Szolnok County. The night was too dark and too cold for staring through windows, but the writer of books stood in front of the glass doors of my bookshelves as though he was staring at images in the glass of the nearest field and a long line of poplar trees and even, perhaps, an image of the first field behind the poplars and an image of a sweep-arm well or of the place where an image of a well might have been.

The man standing in front of the bookshelves said he was a simple man who had never written about anything that he had not seen and who saw only what was in front of his eyes. He had never seen ghosts of men and women or ghosts of libraries. He had never seen, nor would ever see, Tolna County or the Sio and the Sarviz trickling side by side before they meet at last. He had never seen, nor would ever see, Tripp County or the Dog Ear trickling north to meet the White. He had never seen, nor would ever see, Melbourne County or the Moonee Ponds and the Merri trickling. And yet he wanted to breathe with ecstasy, through the curtain of the falling rain, the scent of invisible yet enduring ghosts of places.

He wanted, said the writer of books pretending to be the man from Szolnok County, to see the roadway where long, narrow puddles of cloudy water lie in the wheel-ruts all through the winter.

The water lies for so long in the ruts because the soil is mostly clay. A thick pad of white clay clings to the sole of each of the black boots on the feet of the young woman who walks along the edge of the roadway. She is not so much a young woman; she is hardly more than a child. Her face is pale and faintly freckled. Her eyes are grey-green and her hair is yellow.

He could hardly believe, said the writer of books, that he would dream one day of a ghost of a man walking over the flat land between the Moonee Ponds and the Merri and looking for the ghost of this young woman, or looking for the ghost of her ghost.

For most of today I have stared through my windows at a corner of the nearest field. One of my foremen and a dozen of my farm-servants are planting small bare stems of trees in rows across the field. I suppose my overseer has decided to turn the field into a grove of fruit-trees, but I cannot remember his talking to me about it, and I have not noticed any well for water near by.

My overseer will look after these affairs. For most of the day I was watching the farm-servants, and they were so far away from me that I had to mount my spyglass at the window. I watched a young woman, hardly more than a child. I watched also the sullen young man a few years older who had begun to watch the young woman. Later in the day I began to watch also the foreman, who had begun to watch the other two.

Fewer clouds than usual were drifting across the sky over my estates. The season is spring. When I opened my window and aimed my spyglass, a warm breeze blew against my face. The sun never shines on these windows but it shone all morning on my fields. At midday when the farm-servants stopped to rest. I saw the young woman walk deep into the shade of the poplar trees. The sullen young man followed a few paces behind her, and the foreman watched them both.

I have watched the young woman on other days. I have watched her walking in and out of the white-walled cabin where she lives with her parents and her brothers. I first began to watch her on a day like today in the spring of last year – or it may have been another year.

If you could have watched me, reader, from the day when I first began to watch her, you might have supposed I was watching for the calves of her legs to become rounded, for the bones of her hips to spread apart, for the mounds of her breasts to become apparent behind her clothing, for a look of knowingness to settle on her face. And now, when all these have appeared, you may suppose, reader, that I watch her with pleasure.

I have watched her well. I was still watching her today when the sullen young man among my farm-servants stepped in her way and pretended to stumble against her. I was watching when my foreman called her into the shade of his own poplar tree and when he gripped the bare flesh of her arm, pretending he did it absently, and when he said something with his face close to her face, looking around him as though he spoke about trees or soil.

I was still watching when the foreman had turned away, and when the young woman had stepped over to sit with the other female farm-servants in the shade of the poplar trees. I even saw through my glass the stirring of the branches, and I dreamed that I heard the sound of the wind in the leaves.

The girl is far beneath me. I do not know whether or not she can read and write. And yet I watch her, not with pleasure exactly but with a queer mixture of feelings. And until this morning I had thought of myself speaking to her.

I thought I would have done no more than speak to her. I would have had her stand at sundown by the fence around my parkland. She might have stood well hidden under the green and shaggy branches of my Chinese elms. After night had fallen, my most trusted servant would have led her by way of private passages towards this very library. And here I would have questioned her closely.

I was about to write the words: *This is a strange confession I am making to my editor*...I was on the point of forgetting that all these pages will lie one day on the desk of Gunnar T. Gunnarsen, scientist, in the Calvin O. Dahlberg Institute of Prairie Studies.

I have been writing about myself dreaming. I have been writing only to confuse you, Gunnarsen. I have confessed nothing. Read on, Gunnarsen, and learn what kind of man I am in fact. Read the true story, forger.

I am not a tyrant. The overseer of my estates or the overseers beneath him or the foremen beneath the overseers – those may be harsh men, but I do not oppress. I have sometimes lightened the load of a widow or an orphan who has pleaded with me. Only one thing I will not be refused. If I ask for any young female farm-servant to be waiting at nightfall by a certain gate in the fence around my park, then that female must be waiting alone when my servant calls for her.

I do not ask in my own person. I transmit my message through one or another of my overseers. The stern man taps at an elbow with the butt of his riding-crop. The young female lowers her head. My overseer mutters a few words. The young female keeps her head lowered; she has heard and understood.

If I wondered about such matters, I might ask myself how many a young woman, when she first hears my instruction, supposes that the man she will visit by night is my overseer. I have no doubt that each of my overseers and my foremen chooses certain young females for himself, and that this is well known among the farm-servants. The fathers and the brothers of the young females shake their fists behind the backs of the overseers, or else they joke about the harsh men. Nobody looks towards the windows of this library. If the young women who visit this library keep silent afterwards, as all of them swear to do, then I remain hidden. Here at this table I hide safely behind other men.

I am writing to you now, Gunnarsen, because I no longer dream of my pages coming into the hands of a young woman.

I am writing about the young females on my estates so

that you will wonder, Gunnarsen, what else I have done that I have not yet told you about.

But you will write an answer for me from your suite of rooms in the Institute of Prairie Studies. You will write to me about a young woman I have never seen nor will ever see. You will write to me about a young woman who has never seen nor will ever see the Great Alfold but who breathes with ecstasy, through the curtain of the falling rain, the scent of invisible yet enduring lands sloping gently between the Sio and the Sarviz.

But then I will write to you again, Swede scientist. I will write to tell you what the young females have told me when I have questioned them in this very library, on nights after I have bolted the doors and after my trusted servant has prepared the couch in the adjoining room that I call my study and after the same servant has brought into the library the silver salver and the bottle of wine and the drinking glasses. I will write to you about the young females in the days even before I first saw them walking in and out of their white-walled cabins or planting trees in corners of my fields or scraping dung out of my cattle barns. I will write to you about mere children: boys and girls together on the banks of trickling streams.

I will write such things to you, Swede – I will write such things to you in your Institute with the walls of dark glass that if you are a man in any way like myself you will shut yourself in a room that resembles this library; you will shut yourself away and you will write on pages like these pages of mine; you will write to a young woman who once lived in your own district of America but who lives now far away from you, beside her dream-prairie in a county that neither of us can name.

It was her face that first attracted me. I watched her face for day after day, long before I first looked at her body.

For much of my life I have listened to drunken men talking about the body: 'And then I did this or the other to this or that place on the body...' If any man questioned me I said this or the other about this or that place on the body. It is easy to say such things when all bodies are so much alike. But I would never have spoken about a face.

She pushes open the door in a white wall of her parents' cabin and walks towards me under the dark-green leaves and the bunches of red berries of an evergreen tree whose common name I have never learned. She does not see me; I am well hidden from her.

She passes by me. She is so close that I could look into her eyes and suppose they looked into my own eyes. I have looked into her eyes on other mornings but today I look at the red mark on the clay path behind her. She has stepped on a small cluster of fallen berries, and the thrust of her foot has burst open the fruit and has squeezed out the red pulp and the yellowish seeds and has smeared them together on the path.

I am still thinking of her face, but my thinking leads me by way of many places. I am thinking of the large house, not quite a manor-house, where my uncle and my aunt live with their three daughters, my cousins. The eldest daughter, who is sixteen years old, is holding my hand and leading me around the garden. She is trying to teach me the scent of each flower. I am not more than seven years old.

My cousin leads me to a small shrub in a dark corner and tells me that the pink and white flowers have the sweetest scent of any plant. She tells me that the shrub is a daphne.

I step forward and put my face to the daphne, although I do not expect to smell it. I have already learned that flowers have no scent for me. But I step forward so as not to disappoint my cousin, who has a pretty face. I have already begun to judge young women by their faces.

I am still pretending to enjoy the daphne, but now my cousin takes out from her clothing a tiny pair of scissors and cuts a spray of leaves and flowers from the bush. She forces the stem of the spray into a buttonhole below her throat. Then she kneels on the lawn and puts her arms around me and draws my head towards her so that my nose is almost touching the pink and white bunch of the daphne on her chest.

I do not want to tell my cousin that I cannot enjoy the daphne, but she seems to suspect this without my telling her. With one hand she presses my head against her chest, and with her other hand she drags me forward from the waist so that I stumble against her.

I still believe my cousin is holding me so that I can learn

the scent of daphne. I try to tell her that my nose is a long way short of the flower: that the flower is being crushed between my forehead and her chest I try to explain this, but by now the young woman is holding me so that I cannot speak.

My cousin sends me away and I walk towards the large house. The time is early on a Sunday afternoon. I walk into the passages of the house and then out to the lawns and the flower-beds at the rear. The people of the house are looking at their clocks and expecting visitors, but I am remembering the daphne below my cousin's throat and regretting that I could not look at her face while her arms were around me.

The first short shadows of the afternoon are on the lawns behind the house. I stand in the shadows and I look out, just as I stand and look out from the shadows of this library today.

I stand at the shaded, quieter side of a many-roomed house. Far away behind me at the front of the house, the wide driveway encircles a lawn where a fountain froths above a shallow fish pond. The sun shines on the lawn and on the white water and the green water and on the people coming and going. I know the names and the faces of the people, but what concerns them does not concern me. From where I stand I have seen already what is going to happen to the sunlight that makes the people so cheerful.

While the people of my cousin's family are standing on the wide steps of white marble at the front of their house and waiting to welcome the man who will marry my eldest cousin a year later, I am staring at a poppy-plant. The hairy stem and the lobed leaves are below the surface of the shadow cast by the house, but the flowers reach into the light. The petals are an unusual colour between red and orange.

I would like to ask somebody the name of the colour of the petals. But I do not want to be told that the colour is red or orange, or even that the colour is orange-red. I would prefer to discover that the colour has a name known only to a few people.

This is the day when I begin to learn that the colours of things appear more truly if I look at them from out of shadow. And on this day I begin to learn also that most of the colours of things have no names but that someone such as myself might follow all his life the winding and branching paths of all the colours he has seen or remembered himself having seen.

Now my thinking leads me from the colour of the petal on the poppy-plant to the colour of the jelly where the seeds are embedded in a tomato-fruit. I see large drops of the jelly, with unripe seeds still inside, sliding and then clinging and then sliding again from the lower lip to the cleft of the chin of the same cousin who pressed me against her only weeks before.

I have walked quietly into the kitchen of the house. My cousin and her mother and other older women are watching the servants preparing hampers of food for an outing to the bank of a stream. My cousin, who is now engaged to be married, has been eating a sandwich of salad vegetables. One of the women has said something that has made my cousin laugh and blush. My cousin has pressed the sandwich between her fingers and has burst it, and has gone on laughing. The colour of the poppy on the day when my cousin pressed me against her – that same colour trickles now from the young woman's mouth and down her chin.

All my life I have been so fastidious that I prefer to eat alone rather than watch other people putting food into their mouths. While the picnic-party was leaving for the bank of the stream, I was at the rear of the house, hiding between the rows of red-currant bushes and trying to vomit.

I notice the red mark on the path behind her, and then I notice protruding from under the sole of her boot a cake of the pulp and the seeds of berries and of white clay. On another day this might have been my pretext for speaking to her. I would have told her to look down with her green eyes at the red and the white: at the seeds crushed against the clay.

But this is not the day when I first speak to her. This is one more of the days when I look at her face.

Her skin, of course, is quite smooth and unflawed. On the day when I first saw her I satisfied myself that her face had no scar or blemish. If I had seen even a small mole

I would not be writing about her now. And yet I allow her the scattering of faint freckles on her forehead and across the bridge of her nose. The freckles do not mar the smoothness that I insist on. The freckles lie just beneath the surface.

Her skin is pale and ready for me to mark. I would never mark her skin boldly as another sort of man would mark a white page with black, or as still another sort of man would cause the pink of blood to spread beneath her skin. I may not mark her paleness for some time. I may go on writing what I might have done before I begin to write what I have done.

I look at the eyes of her face. Their colour is peculiar to themselves, but for convenience I call the colour green.

Some people have said that an eye is a window, but anyone who has looked carefully has seen that an eye is a mirror. If I look at an eye in this face that I am writing about, I see only the red roofs of my manor-house and the white walls and the windows reflecting fields and grassland. And if I look closely I see, on the other side of one of those windows, a man sitting at a table and writing.

That man has learnt nothing from looking into eyes. He sees in eyes nothing that he has not seen long before. Yet he goes on looking for a face of a certain kind and he goes on writing that he would like to look through the eyes of that face as though an eye is a window. He goes on looking for a face and he goes on writing as though the eyes of that face are the windows of a room with books around its walls, and in that room a young woman sits writing.

I have begun to write as though Gunnar T. Gunnarsen will send my pages to one of the rivals of my editor. I am writing as though the scientist and forger will take my pages to a room I could not have dreamed of in the towering Institute in Ideal. Gunnar T. Gunnarsen delivers my pages into the hands of a young woman from Lincoln, Nebraska, and I wonder what kind of alliance my enemy has made with this woman who is going to pretend to be my editor.

When I last saw this woman she was trailing her hand in the water of a fish pond on the far side of the prairie that looks like a lawn between Tripp County, South Dakota, and Lancaster County, Nebraska. She was pretending to reach with her hand for one of the red fish that drifted sometimes up to the surface of the pond. She had dipped her hand into the water when the sun was shining on the pond and on the prairie that looked like a lawn. But then a cloud had drifted in front of the sun, and when the woman looked down she could no longer see the tips of her fingers. She thought of a large fish tearing at her fingers with its teeth, and of her blood clouding the water in the ornamental pond.

The woman drew her hand out of the water. Around the white skin of her wrist was a thin line of green. The woman held out her wrist in the sun to dry but she did not rub away the green, and she was left with a dried trace of dark-green that would soon become black.

The woman sat beside the shallow ornamental pond in Lancaster County and stared at the line on her skin. She remembered the story of Winefride in the book of saints she had read as a child.

Winefride was left alone at home on a certain Sunday while the rest of her family were at church. A man named Caradoc arrived at her house and demanded to know where Winefride's father kept his money. Winefride would not tell him, and Caradoc then threatened to cut off her head with his sword. Winefride began to run towards the church, but Caradoc chased her and caught her and drew his sword and beheaded her.

At the place where Winefride's head struck the soil, a crack opened and water flowed out. The flow increased, and the stream of water met the congregation as they were leaving the church. The priest and the people followed the stream towards its source and found Winefride's body with the head lying beside it; near by they found Caradoc, who was rooted to the spot.

The priest placed the head against the neck, the people knelt and prayed, and Winefride was brought back to life. The crack in the soil widened and deepened and became a well, famous for healing. Caradoc was struck dead from heaven. Winefride lived a normal life afterwards, except that a thin red line was always visible around her neck.

GERALD MURNANE

When the woman from Lincoln, Nebraska, had first read as a child the story of Winefride, she had found in the book of saints a picture in which Winefride was no older than herself. The child Winefride was barefoot and wearing a simple tunic that hung to her knees. She was looking up at Caradoc, who was twice her size and was frowning down at her.

The woman beside the fish pond remembered herself as an older child reading her book of saints on an afternoon of bright sunlight in her father's library and seeing behind the pages not a child and a man frowning at her but a young woman and a man who had fallen in love with her. When the girl in her father's library held the pages of the book open in front of her, she read the story of the child who had been beheaded and had come back to life. But when the girl had closed the pages and had put the book on her shelf below her father's shelves, she saw for the first time a space lying behind the spines and the covers of books; and she saw somewhere in that space a young woman who died but was not brought back to life, a man who was rooted to the spot but was not struck dead from heaven, and a well that was full of water but would heal nobody.

The older child grew into a young woman in Lincoln, Nebraska, and kept to her father's library. Sometimes a man would visit the library and would fall in love with the young woman. The man would walk with the young woman between the Platte and the Big Blue, but the young woman would not die and the man would not be rooted to the spot, and afterwards the young woman would go back to her father's library.

Each year while the woman kept to the library, the shelves reached higher above her and the space behind the books seemed wider. When I first saw the woman she was sitting by the ornamental pond, but in her own eyes she was in the space behind books. She had come out from her father's library into the space behind books, but soon she would go back to the library. Soon she would see all around her the shelves of books like the walls of a well, and in the space on the other side of the coloured spines the winds of the world would whistle over great plains and great alfolds.

Now the prairie-scientists have persuaded the woman to travel from the valley of the Platte to the trickling Dog Ear and to pretend to be my editor. Gunnarsen and his gang have told the woman she will soon read the words of a man who is rooted to the spot and will soon be struck dead from heaven in a place where a young woman has died and will soon be brought back to life.

The woman from Lincoln, Nebraska, is pretending to be my editor, but I cannot believe she takes her orders from prairie-scientists. I cannot believe that a woman who has learned all her life from the pages of books would listen to men who live on the other side of books.

If you are still reading my words, Gunnar T. Gunnarsen, take notice that these are my last words to you.

I used to believe that you hated me, Gunnarsen, but now I believe you have hardly thought of me in all the time while I was writing. You have hardly thought of me because you seldom step inside the book-lined rooms of the Institute of Prairie Studies. For most of your life you are out on your grasslands, you and your fellow scientists, counting stalks or measuring the thickness of bushes or pointing your cameras at nests and eggs of ground-dwelling birds. I see you now, stepping carefully among your little bluestems and sniffing with your powerful noses the scents of every kind of small flower. I hear you telling one another in your scientists' language that this or that hillside or hollow is now indistinguishable from virgin prairie.

The young women stand at the windows of their rooms in the Calvin O. Dahlberg Institute. The young women see you at your work far out on the plains of grass under the drifting clouds. You yourselves cannot see the young women, but you are not anxious to see them. You look towards the tall building with hundreds of windows full of images of clouds, and you have no doubt that a young woman stands behind every window and looks out towards you.

Perhaps you do not even know, Gunnarsen and you others, that one at least of those young women calls the grassland her dream-prairie. Perhaps this is one thing that I know and you do not know, because one of those young women once wrote to me. But you would hardly care about such things; you have all those grasslands to study and all those young women to look out at you.

In the heat of midday you rest from your work. Out on your prairies the largest shrubs cast shadows where a man may lie full-length. You lower your bodies among the tussocks of grass in the patches of shade and you rest from your scientists' work. For the time being, you are well out of sight of the windows of the Calvin O. Dahlberg Institute. You are even out of sight from one another in your shaded hollows among the grass; and around the bodies of some of you the vigorous plants of the prairie have already sprung back into place, making you seem to have tunnelled or even to be lying in graves.

You are bothered no more by the heat of the sun. You are resting on the dream-prairie of all the rivals for the position of editor of *Hinterland*. If ever I should envy you, prairie-scientists, I should envy you now.

You begin to talk. Your words drift from one to another of the shaded places beneath the surface of the grass. You talk about young women, some of them hardly more than children. You talk about yourselves as young men and about the young women who once lay beside you in out-of-the-way parts of grasslands – by back roads or railway-lines or even in the neglected corners of graveyards.

And now you talk about children: young males and females not quite young men and women. You are not shy of talking about children. You are prairie-scientists and you presume to talk about whatever has happened on the grasslands of the world. And so you talk about the female children who leaped with you into pools in the trickling streams in the districts where you were born and who sat with you afterwards naked on the sandbank-islands where dragonflies paused above broad beds of rushes. You talk about the female children who taught you what you would do to their bodies in the following summer or what you would do to other bodies after you had come back to the sandbank-islands in the following summer and had found only the beds of rushes and the dragonflies flitting, because the female children had turned into young women and had gone off with young men.

You go on talking, all you scientists of prairies and husbands of editors and of rivals for the position of editor. You go on talking in your tunnels under the prairie of Ideal, which is also the dream-prairie of a young woman who once wrote to me. And I hate you because you rest so comfortably under the swaying grass and you talk so easily about the female children who turned into young women.

I think now, Gunnarsen, that you hardly think of me or wonder about me. You hardly wonder whether I strolled with Anne Kristaly in Tolna County many years ago or whether Anne Kristaly and I sat as children together on our sandbank-island in the trickling Sio or the wandering Sarviz from the north. And if you hardly wonder about me, Gunnarsen, then you would not have forged my editor's name on a letter to me.

If Gunnar T. Gunnarsen did not forge my editor's name, then the forger is one of all those men and women who sit in book-lined rooms in the Institute of Prairie Studies and whose names I will never know.

Even in the Calvin O. Dahlberg Institute, with all that glass for its walls and all that sky around it, some rooms are shut away from the light. Each day, on some higher level, one of those men who prefer to make no show of their power turns away from the outer sunlit rooms and into the corridors leading towards the heart of the Institute. All day in his room where the soft light never varies and where no movement of air lifts the corners of pages, the man guards manuscripts and precious books of the history and lore of prairies.

The man is not an old man, but he is clearly older than Anne Kristaly Gunnarsen. And he has fallen in love with the young woman who might have been my editor. Each day the man invites Anne Kristaly Gunnarsen to his inner suite and shows her his treasures: his carefully guarded pages.

I do not know what my lost editor sees in that man's books, but I know that none of the pages I might have sent her could equal his pages in her eyes. What could I have written and sent from the Great Alfold to lie beside his maps and colour-plates and handwritten texts? He sits with her in a cone of gentle light in one of the huge, hushed rooms of his darkened suite near the heart of the tower of tinted glass on the grasslands of Ideal. He takes her hand politely but firmly. He brings her fingers gently towards a central zone on a page as soft as her own skin. He and she lean forward with their heads close together while they search for a dot that stands for a town such as Ideal. Or he traces with one of her fingertips the line as delicate as a strand of hair that stands for a stream trickling from a lake or wandering from the north. Or he obliges her to lean far across him and to tilt her chin and to watch while his own fingers follow the peaks and ridges of a watershed.

On days when maps have seemed to tire the young woman, my enemy puts away the atlases somewhere outside the cone of light and then comes back from the darkness holding in front of him with two hands a book more bulky than any in my poor, disused library. No man, the young woman thinks, could carry such a weight outstretched in front of him, and yet this man from his dark caves of books has staggered towards her under the weight of his prized volume and has laid it in front of her and has offered to show her its secrets.

What does my enemy uncover now that will make the young woman quite forget the pages I was going to send her? Colour-plates of birds or plants, perhaps, or of mansions and manor-houses much more grand than mine. Plovers, quail, bustards, and all the doomed kinds of bird that scrape nests in the soil; chokeberry, fleabane, and plants nearly all ploughed under – all these my lost editor stares at. Or she stares at the hundreds of windows in colour-plates of enormous houses on vast estates, and she wonders which row of windows looks out from the huge library, and she even seems to forget her own dream-prairie while she dreams of what she might see in pages of the books in that dream-library.

My enemy, I see now, is a man from the archives of the Institute of Prairie Studies. He has so many books of colour-plates and lithographs and woodcuts to show to the women he invites to his rooms that none of those women could want to read afterwards my story from the Great Alfold.

And yet my enemy may be somewhat afraid of me. He has paused among his priceless collections to think of me here at this table with only scribbled pages around me. And in the stronghold of the Calvin O. Dahlberg Institute of Prairie Studies he has devised a plot against me.

The man sits with his many-coloured pages in front of him. Beside him is one more of the young women who dream of being editor of *Hinterland*. The only sound in the room is the rubbing of silk against paper or of silk against silk as the young woman moves a sleeve across a page or unfolds her legs in order to lean towards a far corner of a map, or to study the patterns in the mottled wing feathers of a quail. The man would seem to be quite safe from me, and yet he may be somewhat afraid. He may be afraid, as I wrongly thought Gunnarsen was afraid, that I have something to tell.

What I have written seems now only a scattering of pages. I first began to write because I felt a heaviness pressing on me and because I could not decide whether I remembered a certain thing or whether I dreamed of the thing, or whether I was neither remembering nor dreaming but only dreaming of myself doing one or the other. Perhaps also I was writing because Anne Kristaly Gunnarsen had begged me to send her some of my pages from the Great Alfold. But I soon understood that the woman I had called my editor might never read any page I sent to her and that she might well have supposed I had died.

I am still writing in my library in my manor-house. My enemy of enemies in the Calvin O. Dahlberg Institute is still waiting to read what I have written about Anne Kristaly Gunnarsen: about the woman I once supposed I was writing for.

In fact I know less than my enemy knows. But he would never believe this of me. In fact I have never seen, nor will I ever see, Tolna County; I cannot even breathe, through the curtain of the falling rain, the scent of invisible yet enduring beds of streams. But my enemy would never believe me if I wrote this. My enemy is afraid of me. He knows that whatever I write he cannot contradict. Poring over delicate tints on the paper as soft as skin behind locked doors in the depths of the Calvin O. Dahlberg Institute, my enemy flinches when he thinks of elaborate sentences that a man in my position might challenge him to read. Tracing with limp wrist and gliding fingertip the loops and doublings-back of some broad prairie river on its prolonged route to the Missouri, my enemy cringes when he thinks of having to read long paragraphs of mine in which all names of streams have been changed or the rivers of America have been diverted in their beds or the whole of the Great Alfold has been forced into a strip between the Dog Ear and the White or, worst of all, the dream-grasslands of South Dakota have drifted even he cannot tell where. Driven by the plainness of his native district to look deeply into any place admitting of penetration, my enemy will ponder my prose well.

I am writing about myself
standing in the garden of a large house – but by no
means a manor-house – between the Hopkins River
and Russells Creek. Perhaps my reader is wondering
where Russells Creek and the Hopkins flow, and how far
away those two streams are from the Dog Ear and Ideal.
And yet, whatever atlases I refer to, my reader will still
think the worst. He will think I am writing about myself
standing among gentle slopes and peaceful hills in Tolna
County, or even on the plains of Szolnok County.

I am not sorry for you, reader, if you think of me as
deceiving you. I can hardly forget the trick that you played
on me. You allowed me to believe for a long time that
I was writing to a young woman I called my editor. Safe in

the depths of your glass-walled Institute, you even had me addressing you as reader and friend. Now, you still read and I still write but neither of us will trust the other.

Trust me or not, reader, but whatever I write about myself having done, I will always write about places. I will name the streams on either side wherever I am; I will match landscape with landscape.

I am writing about myself standing in a garden between the Hopkins River and Russells Creek. How can I show you the way, reader, from Ideal, South Dakota, to the few steep, coastal hills between the Hopkins and Russells Creek? Perhaps, you think, the way leads downstream along the Dog Ear, downstream again along the White, and then on down the Missouri. But that way leads towards the sea, as you well know, reader. And you in the place where *Hinterland* will issue from and I who first wrote to you from such an utterly landlocked place as the Great Alfold – you and I are not going so readily towards the sea.

Perhaps the way ought to lead us across the Missouri before it widens. I have looked ahead, reader, and that way is promising. I have looked ahead and seen in Minnehaha County, at the eastern edge of South Dakota, the town of Baltic. From there I looked further east and into the state of Minnesota. I saw in Nobles County the town of St Kilian, and I remembered at once another town far away over my right shoulder: the county seat of Rock County, Nebraska. I remembered Bassett, and the church called St Boniface's. I had found all of these places long before today. But only today I found for the first time still another of the dream-sites of America. I found in Lincoln County, Minnesota, the town of Balaton.

Yet the way leads in another direction, reader. Look up from your Institute to the north, where Virgin Creek trickles into the Missouri in Dewey County. Or start again from Ideal, and look west along White River to the town of Interior. Or follow Cheyenne River upstream from where it joins the Missouri. Follow it past Cherry Creek and much further upstream into Fall River County, South Dakota, and all the way to the town of Oral.

Yes, reader, the way leads upstream, but along much deeper streams than Virgin Creek or Cherry Creek or even the Cheyenne as far as Oral. Two hundred kilometres south of Ideal is the valley of the Platte in the state of Nebraska. By now, reader, you must be used to my looking for signs in districts lying between two streams. You will not be surprised if I ask you to follow the Platte upstream to Lincoln County, where two streams branch – one to the north-west and the other to the south-west.

Reader, we will not follow the North Platte, as one of the branches is called. I have looked that way and seen no signs for us. Follow me, reader, south-west along the South Platte.

You have suspected, reader, for some time, that we are drifting towards the Great Divide. Myself, I prefer the word *watershed*. We are a long way now from the grasslands around the Institute of Prairie Studies; we have come a long way from Ideal. We are almost within reach, we feel, of the watershed of America. In fact, reader, the South Platte will lead us, by a long and tiring route, to the state of Colorado, and into Park County, and almost to Climax.

By some means or another, reader, we have passed Climax and we are no longer in Colorado. Alert as you are, you would have noticed earlier the word coastal in a passage connected with the place where I once stood in a garden. Having found yourself on the other side of Climax, and having read my word coastal, you expect to find yourself drifting towards the sea.

And so you are, reader. Along with myself, you are drifting further away from the peaks around Climax – from the watershed of our huge land. But do not trouble yourself about the sea; do not ask for names of coasts or bays or such things. The land itself is so vast and so richly patterned with streams and towns and prairies that I will never have time for sea. Be content to know, reader, that our journey upstream from Ideal and over the watershed or, if you prefer, the Great Divide, has brought us at last to a coastal district or, as I prefer to call it, a district at the edge of the land.

To reach this district from the heights of Climax we might have followed any of hundreds of streams. West of the watershed, the map of the state of Colorado is marked all over with the lines of streams: fine lines waving on the map like sensitive filaments of underwater animals.

You may assume that we followed some of these streams on our way towards the edge of the land. Suppose, if you like, that we followed Gunnison River. Or suppose that we followed the river Dolores, which flows out of Dolores County and then through San Miguel County – where its waters are mingled with Disappointment Creek – and on past the towns of Bedrock and Paradox and Gateway.

Looking, as always, for pairs or larger patterns of streams, I have come to think of us, reader, as having descended by way of the three broadest rivers in the northwest of the state of Colorado: the Green, the White, and the Colorado. The land between those rivers is mostly empty of names of towns, except for the lonely name, on the border of the state of Utah, of Dinosaur.

I am going to write for some time, reader, about myself standing in the garden of a house with walls of white stone and a roof of red iron.

The house belonged to the widowed mother of my father; she lived in the house with two unmarried daughters and one unmarried son. My grandmother's house was the place where I spent a month of my summer holiday during the years when I thought of myself as changing from a boy into a man. My own house, where I lived with my parents, was as far from the house with the red iron roof as the junction of the North Platte and the South Platte is far from Ideal, South Dakota. My own house was in a district of swamps and heaths between Scotchman's Creek and Elster Creek.

I was left mostly alone in the white stone house, and by the time when I had spent my last summer there at the age of twenty, I had walked perhaps ten thousand times around the cracked cement paths and among the flower-beds and arbors and the islands of shrubs laid out in a pattern of fifty years before. I had walked perhaps ten thousand times from the row of agapanthus near the front gate to the fence weighed down with honeysuckle far back behind the house. And at some point on my walk that lasted for nearly a year of Januarys, I learned what sort of man I would be for the rest of my life.

I learned that no thing in the world is one thing; that each thing in the world is two things at least, and probably many more than two things. I learned to find a queer pleasure in staring at a thing and dreaming of how many things it might be.

But I was myself one of the things in the world, and I was not only the boy-man walking on the winding paths of a garden under a clear blue sky in summer; I was also a man who preferred to keep to his room. At one part of one path that I followed, on the shaded south side of the house, between tall fences covered with ivy and dark-green rainwater tanks with orange-red nasturtiums growing out of cracks in the stone underneath, I saw the window of a room where a man who so preferred could sit reading and writing about men who were out in the heat of the sun.

No thing was one thing. Beside every path that I followed, some plant had the look or the feel of human skin. Parts of the flowers of plants had the shapes of parts of men and women. Each thing was more than one thing. The long green leaves bunched around the agapanthus were the grass skirts of women who were naked above their waists. But any one of those leaves, if I put my hand in among them, was the strap of leather that my teachers at school brought down with all the strength of their arms on the palms of boys for punishment.

Some things were things I could not know about. I have never met anyone or even read about anyone who has my peculiar lack in his nose. After I had first learned, as a small child, that I could never know the scents of things, I took to biting off flowers and slitting them with my teeth and pushing my tongue inside them. Sometimes I tasted a drop of nectar but other people, I was sure, enjoyed something much more satisfying. For most of my childhood I went on stripping away layers of petals and grinding with my teeth into the one sour paste the dusty male parts and the sticky female and the hard white beginnings of fruits. But as a boy-man in the garden of the white stone house I no longer tasted plants. I had read in a popular magazine a list of garden plants known to be poisonous, and I had recognised more than one whose flavour was familiar to me. I had eaten their flowers – and a hundred other sorts of calyx and bract and floret – because I was kept from enjoying their peculiar scents.

As a boy-man I had already decided to tell no one in future that my nose was lacking. Some people had thought I was lying about my nose in order to make them curious about me; they had not believed a nose could fail in that way. Other people had pitied me, as though I could feel the loss of something I had never enjoyed. A few people had asked me what comes into my thoughts when I hear talk about scents. I had answered that I think about clouds. Invisible clouds drift through the air above gardens and countryside. Men with sound noses know when these clouds are drifting past, but I must often have stood unknowing under a sky filled with invisible clouds.

Each thing was more than one thing. Nearly every day in January was fine and hot, but in the evening a cold wind blew from the sea. Each evening in the garden I wore sandals on my feet and shorts on my legs but a thick sweater to keep my body warm. My legs felt cool with the wind blowing over them, but they were hot to touch where the sun had burnt them during the day. The skin of my thighs was red from the sun, but if I lifted the rim of my shorts the skin was white.

If I stood at the front gate of the stone house and looked south across the red iron roofs of houses and between the rows of Norfolk Island pines shading the streets, I saw the sea. If I looked north I saw, much nearer than the sea in the south behind me, the first of the paddocks of grass that formed a far-reaching plain. The provincial city with the red roofs and the Norfolk Island pines was called in summer a holiday resort. People in the streets of the city glanced often at the blue water in the south. I preferred to glance in the opposite direction, towards the yellowish grasslands that rose and fell for two-hundred kilometres from the sea-coast to the north-west corner of Melbourne County. The red skin on my legs allowed me to walk unnoticed through the streets of the holiday resort, but I was not interested in the sea. The white skin under my shirt and shorts had not been exposed to the sun since the days when my parents had compelled me to dress in a bathing costume and to sit on the sand of seashores.

On every afternoon of my month in the stone house, except for the rare days of rain, I wore shirt and shorts and straw hat and sandals and I walked from the white house down through the streets of the city to the lawns of buffalo grass and the plantations of tamarisk in the foreshore reserve and caravan park just short of the beach.

The caravan park was filled with rows of tents and caravans, and in every tent and caravan a family was on holiday. Most of the families included at least one daughter. The daughters of about twelve years and younger I considered children; I would not look at them. The daughters of about fifteen and older I seldom saw; they were old enough to wander away to the beach without their parents, or they had already been claimed by young men and had been taken into the milk-bars of the city, or they were even old enough to be alone in their homes far away across the plains while their parents were on holiday. I looked for girls of about thirteen or fourteen. The older girls had been claimed already or they were far away, but I still had some hope for the girls of about thirteen or fourteen.

Every summer when I walked through the caravan park I saw perhaps thirty girls of the age I was looking for. Yet of the thirty I considered seriously no more than three or four. I glanced at each of the thirty girls from under the shade of my straw hat, but only three or four faces attracted me.

Each summer for seven years I walked up and down the rows of tents and caravans among the rows of tamarisks, glancing from out of the shaded zone around my eyes at three or four girls who were too old to play with the children but not quite old enough to have been claimed by boy-men or young men. I glanced at each girl, and sometimes a face attracted me, but even then I went on walking past.

Every summer for seven years I was waiting for a most unlikely event. The father of a girl was going to recognise me. The father of one of those three or four girls out of the thirty was going to call me over to the shade of his tent and to tell me that he remembered me from somewhere. Then he was going to remember that he remembered me from the days when his son and I had played in the same primary school football team on Raeburn Reserve in the district between the Moonee Ponds and the Merri.

You are going to read much more, reader, about the district between the two streams that I named just now. I have named those streams already on other pages, but only as though I named two lines marked side by side on a page. Now I want you to know, reader, that I was born between those two streams. I was born in that district but I was taken away soon afterwards to a district as far from my native district as the district around Kunmadaras is far from the district between the Sio and the Sarviz. Ten years after I had been taken away I was brought back. I was brought back by my parents to live in the heart of my native district between the Moonee Ponds and the Merri. I lived there for two years, reader, and during those years I felt a queer mixture of feelings.

But you may never be persuaded, reader. I assure you that the district between the Moonee Ponds and the Merri is a part of the same America that you have always lived in. But you, I suppose, can only suppose I have changed the names of streams in order to confuse you. You can only suppose I am still dreaming today, even while I write what I am writing, of the Sio, still trickling from Lake Balaton, and of the Sarviz, still wandering from the north.

As for the unlikely event, reader, that I began to write about...In the years when I walked each summer among the tents and caravans, I lived with my parents in a district of swamps and sand at the opposite end of Melbourne County from the district where I had been born. But the father of the girl whose face had attracted me would have lived in my native district between the Moonee Ponds and the Merri. He had lived there, he would have told me in the shade of his tent, since long before the days when his son and I had played football on Raeburn Reserve, and he would go on living there all his life. He took his holidays each year between the Hopkins and Russells Creek, but he lived between the Moonee Ponds and the Merri, which was his native district and his daughter's native district also.

I would have sat with the father in the shade. He would have told his wife and daughter who I was. I would have spoken politely to the wife. To the girl, I would have nodded and smiled. She would have been too young to have remembered me from the two years when I had lived in our native district, and I would have had nothing to say to her for the moment. I would have been patient.

I would have sat with the father under the awning of his tent. Just out of our sight, behind the tamarisks and the marram grass and the few low sandhills, the sea began. But even in my unlikely dream I would not have thought of the sea. I would have been dreaming of myself sitting with the father and with the son – my former football friend – in the shade of fruit trees on a hot afternoon in February. I would have been dreaming of myself sitting with the family I was dreaming of marrying into, in the native district of all of us.

They would never dream of leaving their native district, the father would have told me, in my dream of him that I dreamed while I sat by his tent in my unlikely dream. And he hoped, the father would have said, that his son and his daughter would never leave – not even after they were married. The father would not have said so, but I would have known why he wanted to live always where he lived in my dream of him in my unlikely dream. He would have been thinking of the grasslands to the north and the west of Melbourne County. We would have been sitting among fruit trees on a green lawn in a backyard, but just out of our sight, behind a few streets of houses, the grasslands began.

Each place is more than one place. Whenever the wind was from the north-west we sat under fruit trees on green grass, but our flat native district was on the grasslands where it had always been.

Pardon me, reader, for that last sentence, which I wrote as though the girl and I and her family sat in fact under those fruit trees. My sentences have been growing more and more elaborate. It becomes harder and harder to write about things dreamed of by the young man I had dreamed of becoming. How much easier it is to write that I often visited the house where the girl lived with her family in my native district, and that I talked quietly with the girl for a few minutes on every visit. How easy it is to write that the girl became my girlfriend after two or three years and that no one in the family was surprised a few years later again when the girl and I would sit under the fruit trees on hot afternoons talking about the house we would live in after we had been married.

The house was north-west from where we sat. Out on the grasslands and approaching the house, reader, you would have seen all around you at first only the whitish grass under waves of watery haze. Then, at last, you notice a smudge of dark-green against the white. In time, the smudge appears as plantations and thickets of European trees, and within the dark-green a smudge of red appears. In time, the red appears as the roof of a large house.

You approach the house from among the deep shadows of the European trees, reader. But you are not yet there. The trees are a park or an outer ring of plantations. Inside the zone of trees is one last belt of grassland – a place where the owners have carefully planted all the grasses that once flourished where this dream-place now lies. You cross the last grassland of all. The red roof and the white walls of the house are still partly hidden behind a garden of shrubs and lawns, all surrounded by a fence of tall pickets. On a path behind this fence I am walking in the cool of the evening.

When I had returned from the foreshore each afternoon I sat in the living-room, as my aunts called it, on the shaded south side of the house. I looked through tall windows at a fence overgrown with ivy. The fence hid everything behind it except for a narrow view of sky. I looked into the deepest shade under the ivy. I looked at patches of moss on paving stones. I looked at the shallow cement saucer, brimful of water from the dripping tap. I wanted to stare at dampness and shade so that I could more readily suppose the tall fence had grassland on its other side.

At the mouth of a cave formed by ivy hanging from the grey fence, a bird of white cement pointed a long red, tapering bill upwards into the air. The bird was the European stork from the story that had been read to me at the age of six by my aunt. She had read the story from the thick red-covered book called *The Children's Treasury*, which was still kept in the bookcase with the two glass doors, in a corner of the room whose windows overlooked the moss and the ivy and the cement stork.

A flock of storks like a long grey cloud returns once again from the other side of the world and settles among chimneys and the steep slopes of roofs. From the houses beneath the roofs two boys come out to watch the storks. One boy admires the storks but the other boy throws stones at them. When the storks have hatched their eggs, the same boy throws stones at the naked young birds. But the storks on the roof are the birds that bring unborn human babies to the houses. Later, the storks bring to the house of the boy who had admired them a living baby; but to the house of the boy who had stoned them the storks bring a dead baby.

In the living-room of the stone house I leave the red-covered book on its shelf behind the glass, but I remember a small, greyish line-drawing of the bottom of the deep pool where the storks obtained the human babies.

In the pool the green strands of weeds are

unwavering. No currents or tides disturb the deep water. The pool is far inland, in soil that is mostly clay. If any stream flows into or out of the pool, it is only a trickling stream.

At the bottom of the pool the unborn human babies are arranged as though seated with their backs against an underwater wall. All the babies are plump, with chubby thighs hiding their sex. Their eyes are closed, and the lids of the eyes never flicker. According to the story, the human babies are sleeping. In time, the storks with their long red bills will prod the babies gently awake and will take them up to live on the earth. But even as a child, I thought of the story as having been falsified for reading to children; I thought of all the babies as dead.

Each January, as my holiday passed, I spent more time in the living-room overlooking the stork and the ivy and less time walking through the caravan park. I still looked out for my few chosen girl-women among the tents and caravans, but they seemed, as I knew them better, too frivolous and too eager to follow in the way of their older sisters. I tried not to feel harshly towards them. I asked myself how a girl-woman could be expected to know that a young man walking past with his face shaded by a straw hat was ready to sit patiently under the fruit trees in her backyard, waiting to talk to her about the grasslands that began just inland from his and her native district.

In the last week of January in Melbourne County and

surrounding counties, one day at least is always a day of north winds. On that day every year the wind is so strong and the air is so hot that even the people on beaches or safe among the streets of Melbourne County look up at the sky for the smoke of bushfires inland. And even if no smoke drifts in the sky, the people think of the month of February still to come, with days of hotter air and stronger winds.

I was born on a day when the north wind blew in late February. In the January before that February, in the counties around Melbourne County, bushfires had burned more forests and grasslands and towns and had killed more people than any fires had burned and killed in all the time since Europeans had first settled in those counties. Even when I was born, one month after the fires had burned away, the stumps of trees were still smouldering on mountainsides just outside Melbourne County.

Some places are many more than one place. In the first photograph taken of me, I am a child of three weeks lying in my father's arms while he stands under a fruit tree on a patch of lawn in the heart of my native district between the Moonee Ponds and the Merri. In each year of the past ten, on a day like today when the north wind is blowing, I have looked at that photograph. Nothing in the photograph has changed since the last hot and gusty day when I looked at the patch of lawn and the fruit tree. The child is still blinking against the sunlight; the father still looks down at the child and smiles stiffly. The place where they stand is still the same place on the patch of lawn. But the place where I am has been changed. The place where I stand to look at the photograph is many more than one place. I am standing in one place after another where those men stand who see themselves as a child in the same photograph that I hold in my hand but who were never taken away as small children from their native district. I am standing on one patch of lawn after another under one fruit tree after another and remembering one after another all the patches of lawn and all the fruit trees I have stood under as a child and as a boy-man and as a man in the district where I have lived all my life between the Moonee Ponds and the Merri.

Each year, on a day of north wind towards the end of January, I gave up walking past the girl-women in the caravan park. I had seen enough to persuade me that each of my girl-women would soon allow some boy-man to claim her. Next year when I looked for her she would have joined the young women and the boy-men and the young men on the beach and in a few years she would no longer accompany her parents when they crossed the plains in January.

On the day in every January when I foresaw this, I pulled my hat low over my eyes and turned at last towards the beach. I walked through the first gap that I could find in the windbreak of tamarisks and then I climbed the low dunes and walked along the sand for the first time in a year. I paid no attention to the howling and frothing and blubbering of the idiot-sea. I kept my head down and went on walking until I had found and studied, for ten seconds from under the low brim of my hat as I passed, the body of a female aged between about sixteen and about forty years, wearing only a bathing suit and with her face concealed behind one or more of a pair of sunglasses, a pair of folded arms, a coloured magazine with a picture on the front of a female in a bathing suit, or a straw hat even wider in the brim than my own. Having found and studied this body, I strode to the low building of grey stone which was the men's changing-shed and toilet block. There, in one of the dark cubicles, with the door snibbed behind me and the walls of grey stone in front of me, I closed my eyes and forced myself to dream of doing to the body on the beach what some boy-man or some young man who had never thought of grasslands would do to each of my girl-women in some year to come, while he and she were in my native district between the Moonee Ponds and the Merri and I was in the district of swamps and heaths between Scotchman's Creek and Elster Creek.

On the day near the end of January when I dreamed of a body on a beach, I would stride out afterwards from the building of grey stone and then through the streets of the provincial city and then inland. From the hill where my grandmother lived at the northern edge of the city I would look as usual towards the plains before I turned aside and went in through the gate in the picket fence. On each of those days I walked to the laundry in the backyard of the white house and I hung my straw hat behind the laundry door for another year. Then I went indoors, and during what remained of January I kept to the shaded rooms.

I kept to the living-room, where the carpet was a faded red and a maidenhair fern hung down from each of two bronze jardinieres. I looked into one of the books from behind the glass doors, or I looked into shallow glass-topped boxes at collections of seashells arranged on a frozen sea of white cotton-wool. Or I sat at a window and looked out at the ivy and the European stork while I prepared myself for the year to come. I prepared to assume the look of a man whose girlfriend is for the time being in another country.

At dusk, on one of those days late in each January, I walked around to the side garden outside the living-room. The lights were on and the blinds had not been pulled down inside the room, but no one sat in the armchairs or stood by the bookshelves. I rattled the leaves of the ivy; I pushed the stork back and forth until the cement slab attached to his feet clattered against the flagstones. I turned on the tap, and water streamed into the cement basin and frothed over the edges and flooded the soil around. I made all these sounds as though I could bring to the window the man who was somewhere in the room, sitting calmly at the table and writing to the young woman he loved, who was in another country.

I stepped further back until the overhanging ivy was

like a cave around me. The soil where I crouched was wet from the pouring tap. If the man had come to the window I would have been wholly hidden from him. But the man went on writing out of my view. I saw nothing of him. All I could have heard or seen on such an evening was a sound like a hand scrabbling in the ivy over my head and the dark shape of a bird flying away from just above me. Even in January the blackbirds were still hatching eggs and feeding their young in the hedges and shrubs around the stone house.

In the year when I was fourteen and spending my second January in the stone house, I searched for blackbirds' nests. For three days I peered into every patch of green where a nest might have been hidden. I kept careful count of the nests that I found and of every egg and baby bird.

I cannot remember today whether I began the search for blackbirds' nests on my own part or whether my uncle or my aunts had first encouraged me. It was understood that I was making war on the birds because they damaged the fruit on the trees in the back garden. But it seems to me today that the half-size apples and pears and the small, woody figs were left to fall and to rot on the grass every year. Perhaps I had decided to make war on the blackbirds because they were European and had driven out some of the native birds of the district.

I made war on all the breeding birds and their young. Whenever I found a clutch of nestlings I wrapped them inside a nylon stocking and drowned them in a bucket of water. Each of the blue-green eggs I found I dashed against a brick wall in a far corner of the backyard. I inspected every smashed egg and counted the unhatched young I had destroyed.

I reported my tallies to my aunts, and they paid me a penny for every drowned baby-bird and every spilled embryo. I reported my tallies honestly, and if my aunts had asked I was ready for them to have counted the dead bodies, both hatched and unhatched. But I was anxious to keep the women from seeing those eggs that had only a blob of bloody stuff in them, even though I had already spread the blob and stirred it with a twig so that I could admire the band of rich orange where the blood-colour met the yellow of the yolk.

I was not anxious to hide the hatched birds that I had drowned, or the birds that were still unhatched but had recognisable bodies. The whole or the almost-whole corpses with naked bellies and with eyelids bulging like black currants and grinning mouths of creamy rubber — these might only have made my aunts think of birth. But the blood-stains mixed with the yolks, I thought, would have made the women think of fertilisation.

I had found in the bookcase in the living room, in the summer when I was thirteen and spending my first holiday in the stone house, a volume bought from a mail-order bookseller, with the words *Famous Artists* in its title. (My aunts kept mostly to the house and were often seen clipping coupons from newspapers or signing for parcels at the front door.) The plates in the book were the first large coloured reproductions I had seen of paintings. Every day before my walk to the caravan park I studied the landscapes and the nudes.

The landscapes, with deep shade under the trees and with streams trickling and clouds drifting, belonged in my own dream-landscape: in the place where I was going to live one day, with alternate bands of white grass and green trees around a house with a roof of red iron.

The nudes repelled me. The skin of the women was yellowish; their bodies were too plump. The fabrics beneath the reclining bodies were too richly crimson or purple, and the carefully arranged wrinkles in the fabrics made me resent the wealth and the power of the men of Europe, who could order their female servants to pose naked for hours and afterwards to set in order the same vast beds that earlier they had been commanded to disarrange artfully and then to sprawl their interesting but lumpish bodies on.

Even in the last days of that first January, when I was thinking of female bodies on the beach rather than faces of girl-women from my native district, the nudes did not attract me. Their tinted skins put me in mind of diseases of Europe that were not yet known between the Moonee Ponds and the Merri. I thought of girl-women dying before their time. I thought of some frail membrane bursting inside my own body when I stood in the dark cubicle with the grey walls. I thought of red as well as cream-white bursting out of me. I thought of myself far from my native district and beside the blue-green sea that I hated and with the red and the sickly white of Europe dripping from the walls around me.

But I had seen the colours of Europe only for that one summer. In the following year I walked to the caravan park on the first day of my holiday and afterwards took down from the bookshelf the volume with its cover brown and made to look from a distance like old leather. The landscapes of Europe were still where they had been, but the nudes were gone. One of my aunts had carefully cut out each tipped-in plate, leaving instead of a nude a white page with a tiny trace of glue on it. The title of each painting was printed across the bottom of the page, but above the title was only blank paper with a yellowish crust or scab at its centre.

I looked into the room from under the ivy. I saw on the ledge below the glass doors of the bookshelves numbers of the magazine that was sent to my aunts from New York City. My aunts subscribed to the coloured magazine. They kept the most recent numbers on the ledge of the bookcase and the back numbers behind the wooden doors lower down. One of the jobs that I did every year in return for my free holiday was to carry outside and to burn for my aunts the stack of back numbers from the past year.

The fiery furnace, as my aunts called it, was roughly

circular and reached to the height of my chest. The walls were of grey-white stone blocks with an opening low down at the front for stoking and an opening underneath for scraping out the ashes. The furnace stood in a far corner of the backyard, near the mulberry tree.

On one of the last days of January in each of many years, I knelt on the lawn in the shade of the mulberry tree and tore out pages from magazines and then crumpled them ready for the furnace. Some of the berries were ripe just above me, but I preferred not to touch them. I disliked the stains they would have left on my hands. Once in a while, if I felt especially thirsty, I would gently pick one of the bright-red, half-ripe berries and place it between my teeth. If I punctured only one lobe of the fruit with a corner of a tooth, the tart juice would turn me against all the crop on the tree.

I pushed into the fiery furnace pages I had looked at briefly in the shaded living-room and had meant to look at again. Even in a large house, said my aunts, you ought not to keep stacks of old pages. And so I burned them all – so many pictures and words that if I had stayed in the living-room on every day of my holiday and instead of wandering through the caravan park had turned page after page, I would not have come to the end of America.

On a green hillside in New Hampshire stands a house with enormous windows. Behind the glass a man and his wife and their daughters of thirteen and fourteen look out at treetops red and orange. No harm came to those people on the day when the picture of them was blackened in an instant in the furnace. The flock of grey and white birds over the level yellow paddocks of Kansas, and the red and white barns and the green fields dotted with stones where the man and his wife and their daughter and her husband all work together breeding pheasants in Wisconsin – those people and those birds lived on after I had seen their pictures turned into powdery ash.

The people and the birds lived on, and I could dream of them for long afterwards, but I was sorry that I had not learned the place-names before I burned the pages. I could remember the names of states of America but I would never know the names of the small towns or of the pairs of streams in the districts where the people would live all their lives. I could never write to the girl-women in New Hampshire or the young married woman in Wisconsin.

My aunts would never have asked me to light the fiery furnace on a day of north winds, but sometimes a breeze would be blowing, and a few pages would be lifted out of my hands and wafted across the lawn. I would walk after those pages, putting my feet down carefully among the soft fallen mulberries. Sometimes, when I had caught up with a page, a young woman or a girl-woman would be looking up from the grass at the sky of a district far away from her own. Perhaps I should have spared that one female. Perhaps I should have taken her page's drifting so far as a sign that she ought to be rescued from the fire.

Perhaps if I had kept that page I would have found in the caption beneath the photograph the name of the small town or of the district or the names of the two streams that would have enabled me even long afterwards to send my letter.

But I would have been hurrying, even on mornings when a cool breeze blew, to finish the job for my aunts and then to walk, if only for the last time, among the faces in the caravan park or the bodies on the beach. I may have paused and looked down at the face on the grass, but I did not spare her, wherever she lived.

I am far from having forgotten you, reader. You would be surprised if you knew how close you seem to me just now.

Reader, I may be far from the man you think I am. But who, in any case, do you think I am? I am a man, as you know; but ask yourself, reader, what you consider a man to be.

You can dream easily enough of the body of a man sitting at this table where all these pages have been strewn. The body is not yet old, but certainly it is no longer young, and the belly on the body protrudes a little, and the hair on the head of the body is turning grey at the edges. You can dream of yourself seeing that body, and I was going to write that you can dream of the words that the hand of the body writes on the pages in front of the belly of that body, but of course you do not have to dream, since you are reading this page at this moment.

Do you suppose then, reader, having dreamed and read, that you have learned what I am?

Let me tell you, reader, what I consider you to be.

Your body – whether or not the belly of it protrudes or the hair on the head of it is turning grey, and whether the hand in front of the belly is writing or at rest or busy at something else – your body is the least part of you. Your body is a sign of you, perhaps: a sign marking the place where the true part of you begins.

The true part of you is far too far-reaching and much too many-layered for you or me, reader, to read about or to write about. A map of the true part of you, reader, would show every place where you have been from your birthplace to the place where you sit now reading this page. And, reader, even if you tell me you have lived all your life in a place of books and colour-plates and hand-written texts deep in the Calvin O. Dahlberg Institute – as well you may have lived it – even then, reader, you know and I know that every morning when you first turned your eyes on that place it was a different place. And when every place where you have ever been on every day of your life has been marked on the map of the true part of you, why then, reader, the map has been barely marked. There are still to mark all those places you have dreamed about and all those places you have dreamed of yourself seeing or remembering or dreaming about. Then, reader, you know as well as I know that when you have not been dreaming you have been looking at pages of books or standing in front of bookshelves and dreaming of yourself looking at pages of books. Whatever places you saw at such times, along with all the places you dreamed of yourself seeing, must all appear on the map of the true part of you. And by now, you suppose, the map must be almost filled with places.

Do not merely suppose, reader. Look with your eyes at what is in front of you. All the places you have so far marked have only sprinkled the wide spaces of the map with a few dots of towns and hairlines of streams. The map shows many hundreds of places for every hour of your life; but look, reader, at all the bare spaces on the map, and see how few the marked places still seem. You have looked at places and dreamed of places and dreamed of yourself looking at places or remembering places or dreaming of places during every hour of your life, reader, but still your map is mostly empty spaces. And my map, reader, is hardly different from yours.

All those empty spaces, reader, are our grasslands. In all those grassy places see and dream and remember and dream of themselves having seen and dreamed and remembered all the men you have dreamed you might have been and all the men you dream you may yet become. And if you are like me, reader, those are very many men, and each of those men has seen many places and dreamed of many places and has turned many pages and stood in front of many bookshelves; and all the places or the dream-places in the lives of all those men are marked on the same map that you and I are keeping in mind, reader. And yet that map is still mostly grasslands or, as they are called in America, prairies. The towns and the streams and the mountain ranges are still few, reader, compared with the prairie-grasslands where you and I dream of coming into our own.

I am writing in a room of a house. All over the table in front of me and all around on the floor behind me are pages. On the walls around me are shelves of books. Around the walls of the house are grasslands.

Sometimes I stare out through my window and I suppose that if I set out walking I would never reach the end of grasslands. Sometimes I stare at the bookshelves and I suppose that if I began to read the books I would never read to the end of books. Sometimes I stare at these pages; and pardon me, reader, but what I suppose would place a heavy burden on you.

Luckily for you, reader, you know I was wrong in some of my supposing. You have these pages in your hand and you can see to the end of them. You are reading these pages now because at a certain time in the past (as you see it) and in the future (as I see it) I came and I will come to the end of these pages.

It is easier for you than for me, reader. While you read you are sure of coming to the end of the pages. But while I write I cannot be sure of coming to the end. I may go on with my endless writing here among the endless grasslands and the books that can never be read to the end.

You are a reader of books, reader. You can suppose what a reader would feel in front of a book that is endless. Myself, I do not read books, as you well know. I do hardly more than stare at covers and spines, or I dream of pages drifting. But I am in danger of writing on endless pages.

Read on, reader. I am about to write about myself living on grasslands in your part of the world and a long way from Szolnok County. You may well suspect me of having changed the names of streams only to confuse you. You may suspect me again of writing about the district between the Sio and the Sarviz. But if I do not write what I am about to write, reader, these pages will be endless.

I was born where the Moonee Ponds Creek, trickling from Greenvale Reservoir, finds an unexpected partner in the Merri Creek from the north. They do not join forces. Their wandering journeys across the stony plains and among the low, bare hills might sometimes suggest a coming marriage, or at least a friendly meeting, but they follow their separate ways to the end – the Merri through ever-deeper gorges to mingle with the Yarra above its falls, and the Moonee Ponds through a widening valley into the same swamp where the Maribyrnong and the Yarra also lose themselves just short of the sea. This is my part of the world.

I became in time, and I am still today, a scientist of grasslands, but I have been a scientist of many things.

I was once a scientist of soils. I wanted to know why I had walked with ease as a child on the soil between the Moonee Ponds and the Merri but afterwards I had stepped warily wherever I lived or travelled in other districts of Melbourne County.

As a scientist of soils I first read the words of other soil-scientists. I learned that the thing I had called simply *soil* was in fact hundreds of things – or many more than hundreds of things, according to the scientists of things. I read about the hundreds of things that I had once called *soil*, and I learned what I had been hoping to learn: when I had walked as a child between the Moonee Ponds and the Merri, my feet had pressed against an assortment of things a little different from the assortments of things in other districts of Melbourne County.

I had hoped to learn that this difference came from perhaps ten things: that perhaps ten of the hundreds of things in the soil of my native district were in no other soil of Melbourne County. If I could have read about ten such things I would have gone no further in my studies as a scientist of soils. I would have become a scientist of particular things. I would have called the ten things found only in my native soil my own particular things, and I would have studied nothing but them. I would have tried to learn the peculiar qualities that distinguished my own particular things from other things of other districts. I would have tried to learn from these peculiar qualities how a native of the district between the Moonee Ponds and the Merri ought to live his life. This would have been the hardest part of my studies. I might have had to learn, for example, how a man ought to live if one of the peculiar qualities of one of the particular things in the soil of his native district was that it seemed its rightful shape in darkness equal to the darkness of underground, but that it seemed less truly shaped in daylight or even in the light of a dim room. Or I might have had to learn what a man ought to do as a result of his learning that the smoothest to touch of the same particular things kept its smoothness only while it was damp from the water of underground – the invisible streams flowing through dry-seeming soils.

Or I might have become a scientist of names. Each of the ten particular things would have had to be named, and so would each of its peculiar qualities. I would have given to the things and their qualities solid names that would sound well if I spoke them aloud on the plains of my native district. Of all the sciences I might have studied, the science of names would most have absorbed me. Even before I knew whether or not my ten things existed, I had chosen names that might have suited them.

Here for you to read aloud, reader, are my names for the ten things I had hoped as a scientist to find in the soil of the district between the Moonee Ponds and the Merri. And if you wonder, reader, how the names have come to be in the American language and not in some more heavy-hearted language, then perhaps you are not quite the reader you think you are.

Stainer-of-skin; sourer-of-tongues; yielder-to-rains; resister-of-unseen-streams; shrinker-from-light; mirror-of-nothing; boulder-crumb; tough-in-the-fire; cling-to-all; remembrancer-of-green-leaves.

I used to walk across my native district murmuring these and other such names. I felt the soil of the land between the Moonee Ponds and the Merri sticking to the soles of my shoes, and I supposed I was going to become soon the only man who had names for what mattered most in his native soil.

But my native soil had no things peculiar to it. I learned that the things in soil are only patterns of other things. My native soil was a little different from other soils, but only because the hundreds of things in it were arranged in patterns a little different from the patterns of the same hundreds of things in the soils of other districts.

I thought of becoming a scientist of patterns. I might have studied some of the thousands of patterns that might have appeared among the hundreds of things in the soils in all the districts between all the streams in Melbourne County. Then I might have studied those patterns that appeared only among the things in my native soil. And if I had not learned enough from those patterns, I might have studied the likenesses between them. I might have tried to learn from the likenesses between the patterns of my native district as distinct from the likenesses between the patterns among the things in the soils of other districts.

By now I foresaw myself studying in time even the patterns in the likenesses between patterns. Yet I could not think of walking on the soil between the Moonee Ponds and the Merri and thinking that that soil was that soil and no other soil only because of something in the pattern of certain likenesses between patterns of the hundreds of things in soil.

I remembered how I had been cheered a little by my study of names, and I thought of becoming a scientist of words or even of languages. In the twilight of summer evenings, when the people were resting in their gardens, I used to walk in every part of my native district. I walked past the sprawling villas on the high slopes overlooking the Moonee Ponds; I walked deep in among the walled courtyards of the Old Town; I even crept around the spiked fences of outlying manor-houses by the headwaters of the Merlynston. Whenever I heard the sounds of quiet speech from the other side of a fence or a courtyard wall, I stopped to listen and to make notes. I noted words oddly pronounced or syllables unexpectedly stressed; sometimes I heard a whole phrase that might have been part of a separate dialect of my native language. With all my notes, I might have become a scientist of the depths of languages. I might have learned that a language grows from roots and soil just as grass grows. I might have followed the dialect of my native district down to its roots. I might have studied the soil and even the rock under the language of my homeland.

I should have listened for longer to the murmurings from gardens and courtyards. Behind the hedges of cypress and the avenues of agapanthus in the grounds of the villas facing west across the valley of the Moonee Ponds, behind the rows of iron spikes reaching far back and out of sight around the last remaining manor-houses where the shallow Merlynston begins to trickle from the uplands, and behind the walls of pale brick in the Old Town with moss in their crevices and with scarlet flowers spilling down from urns on their corner-posts – deep in the privacy of their homes, the people of my district spoke in particular ways because the soil-of-speech where the roots of their speech were outspread was a particular soil-of-speech.

I should have studied that particular soil-of-speech, but I became impatient with listening from the shadows of hedges and from behind stone walls and rows of iron spikes. One Sunday afternoon in a certain winter, when the people between the Moonee Ponds and the Merri were indoors in their libraries and when the only figures visible in the bare gardens of villas under the grey sky were stone statues of trolls, I strode away from the houses and into the public gardens and the common lands of my native district. I had become tired of speculating about places deep out of sight: about the roots and the soil of speech and every other sort of root and soil. I had decided that the look and the feel of my native place would be enough for me. I would look with my eyes and listen with my ears and touch with my hands and press with the soles of my feet, and afterwards I would go back to my table to write. I would write what I had seen and heard and touched and felt; and whatever words I wrote I would recognise as being in my native language. Then I would read and study my own words. I would become at last a scientist of my own writing.

On that wintry Sunday afternoon before I turned to go back to my table, I stood on a mound overgrown with spear-grass and marshmallow beside a deserted sports-field. From there I looked west over the clay-lands speckled with the roofs of villages and over the gentle hollows short of the valley of the Moonee Ponds; I looked east over the variegated roofs of the Old Town and then over the moorland towards the Merri; then I looked north where houses and villages became fewer and the grasslands came into view, spotted with reddish stones and with dark-green clumps of boxthorn. I saw on the far side of the grasslands the blue-black ridge of Mount Macedon, which has given me my bearings all my life and which I have looked at from vantage places in many parts of Melbourne County but which I have never visited, so that whenever I see a coloured photograph of one of the mansions of Mount Macedon surrounded by groves of trees with leaves of gold and flame-colour and by thickets of rhododendrons with bunches of pink and purplish flowers, I fail to see how those huge houses and all those coloured leaves and flowers could be arranged inside what has always seemed to me a dark-blue mass of trees native to Melbourne County and adjoining counties, unless the dark-blue is only a cloud that has drifted between me and a district of Europe or Asia.

I looked across my native district towards Mount Macedon. I had thought of becoming many kinds of scientist so that I could think and speak as a man from between the Moonee Ponds and the Merri. But on that Sunday afternoon I only hoped to hear from out of my own mouth a few words sounding distinctively.

I braced my feet among the weeds. I turned my face north-west, and I opened my mouth and waited for the air that had come from counties whose names I did not know and had poured down through the cold, dark-blue hills known as the Central Highlands and had then been shaped into a particular wind on the downward slopes around Jackson's Creek and in the winding valley of the Maribyrnong and at last on the grasslands of my own district. I opened my mouth and waited for the wind to blow my tongue around.

I am not writing by hand on these pages. I am sitting at a typewriter and using the index finger of my right hand to press all keys except the large unlabelled key in the lower left-hand corner for raising the roller to receive upper-case letters or quotation marks, ampersands, and other rare marks.

I do not claim that my way of typing on pages is any sort of distinction, but the only other person I have read of who typed as I do is a character in *Life Stories*, by A.L. Barker, which was published in London in 1981 by the Hogarth Press.

The photograph of A.L. Barker on the dust-jacket of *Life Stories* shows the author to be a woman, although her first names are never used. The book is presented as a collection of pieces of fiction, but between these pieces are passages narrated in the first person by a female narrator; these passages seem to be autobiography. In one of the passages between stories the narrator describes one of her first jobs as a young woman in the late 1930s. She worked for a publishing house in London, in an office where writers wrote and edited pages of magazines meant for what I call elsewhere in these pages girl-women. The magazines were mostly filled with short stories. The narrator of *Life Stories* was surprised to find that the writers of these stories, which were read eagerly by thousands of girl-women in many countries, were mostly men. The writers used female pen-names but they were mostly men and mostly middle-aged, and one of the men composed the final draft of every one of his stories by tapping for hour after hour at his typewriter with one nicotine-stained index finger.

I type slowly and carefully. I stare at the keyboard and I try to see in the air between my face and the keys the words I am about to type. I make mistakes, but I am nearly always aware of a mistake in the instant before I make it. I see the correct letter in the air and then I see the wrong letter in the path of my index finger, but too late for me to stop my finger from pressing on it. The metal hammer flies up and strikes the paper, but I know beforehand that the wrong letter will appear on the page. Yet I do not know at once what the misspelled word will be. My index finger goes on leaping to the last letter of the word before I can pause to read the misspelled word.

I study each misspelled word. I am interested in my mistakes, and I wonder how I came to make them. Sometimes I trace through the air over the keyboard the path that my finger took and then the path that it should have taken, and I wonder why my finger veered onto the wrong path. At other times I read the sentence with the misspelled word as though I am reading a message written by some other man.

Two hours ago, while I was typing a page about my studies as a scientist in Melbourne County, my finger made its usual long diagonal leap from the first to the second letter of the word *soils*. The pad of the finger landed safely on the second letter, but then, perhaps remembering its soaring leap from the *s* to the *o*, my index finger travelled exactly twice the distance needed from the *o*. The finger then made one short and one long hop to finish the word so that the sentence when I looked at it was: *I was once a scientist of souls*.

When I think of a soul I think of a ghostly shape of a body. I think of my own soul as a ghostly shape of my own body. When that event takes place which will cause other people to begin to say of me that I have died, my ghostly shape will have drifted away from my body. Where my soul will have drifted to, I do not know as yet. But perhaps the ghost of me knows a little more than I know. Perhaps, two hours ago, the ghost of my index finger nudged aside the finger that I saw hopping and leaping across the keyboard of my typewriter. Perhaps the ghost of me tapped with its index finger at one letter rather than another to tell me that my native district has a soul.

Perhaps my native district has a soul. Perhaps when the grasslands between the Moonee Ponds and the Merri have been covered over by roads and houses, and when the two streams themselves — the trickling stream and the stream that wanders from the north — have been turned into concrete drains, then my district may be said to have died, and its ghost will have drifted away from it. And perhaps one day in the country of ghosts my own soul — my own drifting ghost — will see drifting towards it a ghost with the look and the feel of virgin grasslands between the ghost of the Moonee Ponds trickling and the ghost of the Merri wandering from the north.

If you got up sometimes, reader, from your table deep in the famous Institute, and if you looked sometimes at an atlas instead of at books with colour-plates of birds or of prairie-grasses or at collections of pages from writers in far states of America, you would find in time the name of every place I have named in my pages and of some persons I have not named.

I have already written, on another of these pages, the names of places that you or I might pass, reader, if we travelled first south from Ideal, South Dakota, to the Platte River and then upstream to the junction of the North Platte and the South Platte and from there upstream along the South Platte towards Climax, Colorado, and afterwards towards the district between the Hopkins and Russells Creek. We were not so much interested in the North Platte, reader, but now is the time for me to remind you that we passed, on our way to Climax and beyond, the junction of the South Platte and a river that might have led us to a place somewhat different from Climax, Colorado, and might never have led us to the district between the Hopkins and Russells Creek. In Weld County, Colorado, near the town of La Salle, is the junction of the South Platte and the Thompson. If, at La Salle, we had turned aside into the lesser river instead of following the South Platte towards Climax and further, we would have arrived almost at once in Larimer County, Colorado, and at the town of Loveland.

Having read so often about districts between streams, reader, you may be wondering when I am going to write about the most noticeable of all such districts: the district between the North Platte and the South Platte in western Nebraska. You may be wondering when I am going to mention the strangely shaped district between the two rivers that merge near the town of North Platte in Lincoln County, which is not to be confused with the state capital of Lincoln in Lancaster County nearly three hundred kilometres to the east.

I have only now mentioned that district, reader, but I have been looking at the district or dreaming of myself looking at it for as long as I have been writing on pages. Almost as soon as I began to look at maps of America, I noticed the district that might have been shaped like a female breast if the North Platte and the South Platte had met in Morrill County instead of wandering side by side through four counties and for nearly two hundred kilometres. How could I not have noticed, almost as soon as I began to look at maps, the district that might have been shaped like a female breast but is shaped in fact like a preposterous nose?

And how could I not have wondered often who I might have been if I had been born in the district between the North Platte, trickling from Wyoming, and the South Platte, wandering from Colorado, and what I might have done if I had gone on living on the grasslands of Morrill County or of Garden County or a little further south, in Deuel County, whose chief town is Chappell?

On each Sunday of my child-
hood, the colour that I saw in the silk of the vestments
and the altar-cloths in church was green or red or white or
violet. For one hour each week one or another of those
colours appeared, in strict accordance with the calendar of
the Roman Church.

The colours coming and going were like the threads
that I watched in the hands of the girls during sewing
class, on Friday afternoon in the schoolroom. I sometimes
asked a girl to let me look at the underside of the cloth in
her hands – the side away from the pattern of leaves or
flowers or fruit slowly forming. I trusted that a pleasing
pattern was beginning to appear on the upper side of the
cloth, under the eyes of the girl. But I studied the side of

the cloth that seemed to matter less. I watched the tangled strands and the knots of mixed colours underneath for hints of shapes quite different from leaves or flowers or fruit. I would have enjoyed the game of pretending to the girl that I knew nothing of the pattern she was working at: of pretending to think that the tangled colours were all I could admire.

The colours and the seasons of the Church were complicated, but I saw them only from beneath. The true pattern was on the other side. Under the clear morning sky of eternity, the long story of the Old Testament and the New was a richly coloured tapestry. But on my side, under the changeable skies of Melbourne County, I saw only the green and the white and the red and the violet strangely interlaced, and I made from them whatever patterns I could.

The liturgical year began with Advent, which was a time of looking forward to Christmas. Yet the colour of Advent was not the green of hope but the violet of sorrow and repentance. And although the year was only beginning inside the church in Advent, outside in Melbourne County spring was almost over. At the end of Advent would come the season of Christmas and white for joy. But only a few weeks later, and in the first heat-wave of summer in Melbourne County, the colour would be green again for the season after Epiphany and the looking forward to Easter. The green would persist through the hottest weeks of summer, when bushfires might be burning at the edge of Melbourne County. Then, at the time of year

when I had been born, when the north wind blew at the
end of February, Lent would begin and the same violet
would reappear that had been, in late spring and early
summer, the colour of Advent. Easter, in the mild days
at the end of autumn, was white. The white continued
through the month and a half of the season after Easter
but on Pentecost Sunday, in the foggy first weeks of winter
in Melbourne County, the rare and brilliant red appeared.
After the brief red, the longest of the seasons of the
Church began: the long green sequence of the season
after Pentecost. Even on bleak Sundays in mid-winter the
church was green with the expectation of Christmas, which
seemed then only faint and whitish on the other side of far,
violet Advent.

I thought of all these colours as the underside of the
true and the much more eloquent pattern that was visible
only to the inhabitants of heaven. I was not resentful at
having to look for the time being at the crossed and tangled
strands on the underside of my religion. I even looked
for more knots and quirks. Each Sunday the different
readings from the Bible told part of the story of Jesus,
or the story of the Jews (but only until Jesus had founded
the Universal Church), or the story of the world. The
beginnings of these stories were in Genesis. The one end
of all three stories was prophesied by Jesus in the gospels
and also by John in the Apocalypse. For a week or more
after Christmas, the story of Jesus seemed to go forward at
the slow pace of my own life. Six days after Christmas Day,

Jesus had only just been circumcised; six days after that, the three Wise Men had only just arrived with their gifts. But I could only think this if I ignored the epistles, which were also read on Sundays, and which spoke always of Jesus as dead and gone. Soon, even in the gospels Jesus was thirty years old and wandering with his disciples, and for the rest of the Church year things happened before their rightful time, or the same things happened again and again.

And from the fig-tree learn a parable: when the branch thereof is now tender, and the leaves come forth, you know the summer is nigh.

Each year as a child I heard these words in the gospel for the last Sunday after Pentecost, which was the last Sunday of the Church year.

The number of Sundays after Pentecost in any one year was between twenty-four and twenty-eight. The number was determined by the date of Pentecost itself, which in turn was determined by the date of Easter. These and many other details of the complicated calendar I learned as a boy from studying the table of movable feasts in my missal.

Every Sunday after Pentecost, like every other Sunday of the year, had its own gospel reading: a passage read aloud by the priest first in Latin at the altar and later in our own language from the pulpit. The gospel reading listed in my missal for the twenty-fourth Sunday after Pentecost was *Matthew 24, 1535*. In a year when the twenty-fourth was also the last Sunday after Pentecost, the priest would read the passage from Matthew and I would hear, on the day when the calendar had told me to expect them, the words that made me shiver.

But I much preferred what happened when the twenty-fourth was not the last Sunday. In such a year, on the twenty-fourth Sunday, I would turn to the pages for that Sunday, but I would have learned already from the notes attached to the table of movable feasts that a different gospel was allotted to that day. The notes would have reminded me that the verses from Matthew belonged not to the twenty-fourth or to any other numbered Sunday; the verses belonged to the *last* Sunday, whenever that day happened to fall. And so, on one Sunday, or on two or even three or four Sundays in an exceptional year, I could glance privately at the sentence about the fig-tree, but in the church on that Sunday some other gospel would be read aloud.

Some other gospel would be read aloud in the church, but I would be whispering to myself the words from the twenty-fourth chapter of Matthew, whose hour had not yet come. I would be wondering how I could warn the women with child and those giving suck. Or I would have decided that the young women should not be warned; it was their husbands who should have warned them. I almost preferred the women to suffer as punishment for having become the wives of men who could never learn a parable from any tree.

While I was whispering in church the words that were

going to announce, all in good time, all three of the end
of the ecclesiastical year, the fall of the city of Jerusalem,
and the destruction of the world, the season in the district
between the Moonee Ponds and the Merri was late spring.
The lilac flowers in front gardens had turned brown and
had shrivelled. The magpie fledgling teetered on the edge
of its nest in the sugar-gum high over Ray Street, and the
parent-birds no longer bothered to dive at the heads of
children walking underneath.

Across the road from the church, on the lawns and
pathways of Raeburn Reserve, I could still see the last few
of the small papery discs that had fluttered down from the
elm tree a month before. In the days when the discs had
been drifting down, I had dragged my feet through heaps of
them and had thrown handfuls over my head like confetti.
Sometimes I stopped and examined one of the discs and
saw the red-brown lump at its centre. Then I remembered a
picture I had seen of a dark blur that was a tadpole-embryo
at the centre of a bubble of spawn. I supposed the discs
from the elms were seed-cases and each lump at the centre
was a minuscule elm tree wrapped and curled darkly in on
itself. I was walking among thousands of unborn elms,
arrived before their time or in the wrong place.

In the year when I was twelve years old, on Sundays
when I was already thinking of the fig-tree although the
coming-forth of the leaves had not yet been announced
in church, I used to walk in the afternoon from my
parents' house to a street where the houses ended abruptly

and grasslands began. I walked to Sims Street, which is still marked on maps of my native district although the paddocks of grass that I saw on the northern side of that street have been covered for more than thirty years by streets I have never walked in.

I walked to Sims Street on Sunday afternoons leading a dog named Belle, who was a wire-haired fox terrier less than a year old. My father could never have spared the money to buy a dog such as Belle; he had answered a newspaper advertisement offering pedigreed female pups free to anyone who would give them a good home. Belle was said to belong to all our family but she was kept chained in the backyard and was mostly forgotten by my parents and my brothers. Sometimes when I came home from school I found time to unfasten her chain and to stand watching while she ran in circles around the back lawn. On afternoons when I had other things to do I tried to sneak into the house without Belle's seeing me – I was always ashamed to hear her whimpering for company.

In the autumn after the spring when I had walked with Belle to Sims Street, and after my parents had taken me to live in the sandy district between Scotchman's Creek and Elster Creek, my father announced one evening that we had to get rid of Belle. To use my father's words, Belle had come into season for the first time and we had no place to lock her away from the male dogs of the neighbourhood.

My father was the son of a farmer and was not afraid

to kill animals. He went out into the backyard as soon as it was dark. While he was looking for the tomahawk and a hessian bag, I crept out and patted Belle and said that what was going to happen was not my fault. Belle did not look at me; she was watching two dogs at our front gate.

I was inside the house while my father was pushing Belle into the sugar-bag and tying it around her so that only her head was free, and while he knelt over her and killed her. I heard no noise from Belle, but I heard a frantic barking from the male dogs at the front of the house. When the male dogs stopped barking I thought they must have heard my father hitting Belle on the head with the blunt edge of the tomahawk or even Belle herself groaning or whimpering. But then the dogs began barking again, and they were still barking when my father came inside and washed his hands carefully with the sandsoap in the laundry.

My father told me that Belle had died quickly and without suffering. He said her skull had been as thin as an eggshell and he had only had to hit her once or twice. He said he had buried her in a deep hole that he had dug beforehand. The male dogs would soon go away, my father said. They would smell the blood from Belle, or somehow get wind of her death, and then they would leave us alone. But I thought I heard the two males still outside and sniffing in the dark while I lay in bed that night.

On my walks with Belle on Sunday afternoons in spring, I passed through Raeburn Reserve. For as long as the seeds were lying under the elms I used to scoop up a handful as I passed. I packed the seeds into my shirt pocket until it bulged out from my chest.

After I had turned left into Sims Street from Landells Road I saw that I was walking along a notable boundary. The greyish stripe of Sims Street, which was not a paved street but only a trail of wheel-ruts and puddles, was the border between the town where I lived, which was red-brown from the terra-cotta tiles on the roofs of all the newly built houses, and the green paddocks leading back to the grasslands where I dreamed of living.

Half-way along Sims Street on those Sunday afternoons I unhooked the lead from Belle's collar. She ran far out into the grass and then back to my feet, then far out and back again. While Belle was far out in the paddock I dragged the elm seeds out of my shirt pocket and strewed them just inside the fence on the north side of the street.

I knew the seeds I was scattering were seeds of a tree from Europe, whereas the paddock had once been covered with the trees of my native district. But I had always admired European trees for the deep shade that they cast in summer, and I had often thought how strange it would be to live in a country where the forests were of trees that I had seen only in gardens and parks. Such forests would have seemed more truly wilderness than any bushland in my own part of the world. In the deep shade of a forest of oaks or elms I would have felt a mixture of feelings. I would have felt urged sometimes to do the worst I could do – to lie in wait for the barefoot female child of fairy tales who would soon appear, lost and helpless. At other times I would have felt inspired to search for the castle or the monastery at the heart of the forest, and then for a certain precious book in the library among the rooms and corridors.

At that time, Jesus said to His disciples, When you shall see the abomination of desolation, which was spoken of by Daniel the Prophet...

The world was far from neatly ordered. Colours spilled over what should have been their boundaries. Many a colour had traces of another colour showing through from underneath.

In the streets and gardens of the district between the Moonee Ponds and the Merri the season changed from winter to spring and then almost to summer, but inside the church the one long season of hope persisted. The green of hope seemed appropriate in winter; but September would come, and then October, and the leaves of the elms in Raeburn Reserve would be thick against the sunlight, and yet the Church would seem not to have noticed the dark greens or the emerald greens of leaves or even the orange-reds and the yellows of poppies and roses in front gardens but would still be waiting in its green of hope. And the longer the green of the Church lasted, the more often I thought of the words that had still not sounded from the gospel of Saint Matthew, in which the green leaves of the fig-tree came forth from the grey branches under the grey sky and the smoke of the end of the world.

Late in September each year the air one morning would be surprisingly warm. For two days the sun would have been shining, with a scattering of high, white clouds, but on the third morning the sky would be quite bare and the wind would blow in gusts. The wind would be not the faintly damp wind from the sea but a drying wind from inland – the first north wind of the season.

Long before midday the north wind would dry the dark patches of moisture from the ruts and hollows in streets where the mud had been knee-deep during the winter. All morning the loose soil from the crumbled ridges between the ruts, together with the fine silt from the dried beds of puddles, would be lifted by each gust into the air but then let fall. By lunchtime the wind would have stopped playing about. What had been fairy-puffs and streamers in the morning were now bomb-bursts and continuous pourings upward of clay-loam dried in a day to the fineness of sand. The first dust of summer was blowing in the streets of my district.

On the day of the first north wind in the season of spring, I closed my eyes and felt against my face the weather of high summer. The north wind had brought into the streets and gardens between the Moonee Ponds and the Merri the weather of the plains that reached from the edge of my district north to Mount Macedon and of the wider plains further inland. Before I had been able to prepare myself, before I had understood that the winter had ended, I was breathing the air of the summer that was still to come.

I was standing on a certain page of the calendar, but the hot wind was blowing against my face from a page out of sight. And the calendar that I was standing on was only the calendar for the district between the Moonee Ponds and the Merri: a calendar with pages of the colour of grass or of flowering bushes in front gardens. If I thought of the calendar for the plains further inland and the calendars for the great plains of America and other countries of the world and lying among all those calendars the calendar of the Church with the season after Pentecost like a bright green stripe across page after page, then the colours of the world began to blur.

On the day of the first north wind in spring, in the year when I was twelve years old, I sat near a fig-tree whose leaves were coming forth. On the grey branches the leaves were green: the same hopeful green that I would see in the church for many more Sundays yet. The fig-tree was in the backyard of my parents' house on the flat land east of the junction of the Moonee Ponds and the Westbreen. I looked at the green coming forth from the grey, and I looked at the dust stirring behind the wire-netting of the fowl yard fence. I had not wanted to think of summer, but the north wind had made me think of the summer that was nigh.

I thought of the colours red and dark green. The dark

green was the colour of the water in the fish pond on the square of lawn between me and the back door of the house. The red was the colour of the four chubby fantail fish in the water.

The fish pond was not an ornamental pool dug out of the lawn and overhung by reeds and by fronds of ferns. The square brick pond had been built on the level surface of the yard by the previous owner of the house. The four walls were rough red bricks raised to the height of my thighs and lined with cement. The water in the pond was green. You would see one or another of the fish, surprisingly red, if it drifted up to the surface; but if you reached out your hand, or if your shadow fell across the water, the red flashed and then plunged out of sight in the green.

I had lived in the house in my native district for less than two years. The season I am writing about was only the second spring that I had spent between the Moonee Ponds and the Merri. The house with the fish pond behind it was the first house I had lived in that was owned by my parents. A few months after I was born my parents had taken me away from my native district, and from then until I was ten years old I had lived in rented houses, a different house almost every year, in counties other than Melbourne County.

The house on the clay a little east of the Moonee Ponds was older and uglier than most of the houses around, but it was the first house I was proud to be seen going into. Boys and girls from my school, whenever they passed my house, looked over the front gate, or so I hoped, and thought of a boy in the shade of the apricot tree whose outer leaves they could see at the rear corner of the house. Or the boy that they thought of strolled across the lawn (the first back lawn my father had ever mown) to taste the red currants from the bushes that were only just visible behind the house on its blind side. Or the boys and girls that I thought of thought of the boy beside his fish pond.

The fish pond on the back lawn was well hidden from the street. A few boys from my school had walked around the pond and had leaned over and peered into the green water. Sometimes a visiting boy waited patiently until he saw one of the red fish. One boy had once dipped a stick into the water and had dragged out a tangle of ribbon-shaped leaves and hairy strands of water-plants and had held them, streaming with water, in front of my eyes. But I had not invited that boy to my house again, and even my regular visitors were not encouraged to loiter near the pond.

When I had first seen the pond, on my first day in the house with the apricot tree and the back lawn, I had seen clearly that the bricks went no further down than ground level. The pond was built on the surface of the yard, with the lowest bricks set into the soil to the depth of only a few centimetres. But after a month or two my father's careless mowing had left tufts of grass growing against the lower rows of bricks. I teased the tufts every day with my fingers to hide even more of the bricks. Sometimes

I strolled around the corner from the side of the house into the backyard and tried to catch sight of the pond as it would have appeared to someone visiting my house for the first time. I wanted my visitor to be confused by the unruly grass and to see the pond not as resting on the ground but as protruding from beneath it: as the blunt end of a deep column reaching upwards from a sheath of grass and earth.

In the spring of the year when I was twelve years old I was preparing for the first visit to my backyard of a girl who was the same age as myself and who lived near Sims Street, where the grasslands began, a kilometre north from my house.

Later I will write the name of the street where the girl lived with her parents, but first I have to prepare my reader for what he is about to read.

Did you notice just now, reader, my writing as though you are no longer my reader but only someone I am writing about?

I have written by now on many pages. Each day I cover a page with writing and then I push the page gently away from me towards the edge of my table. By now the table is strewn with so many pages that each page I push away from me causes other pages to drift ahead of it. Sometimes one of those drifting pages drifts over the edge of the table in the way that a cloud drifts over the edge of a district of level land. Sometimes on my way from this table to the window I pass some of the pages that have drifted over the table-horizon. Sometimes my walking past causes the air to move and a page to drift a little across the floor.

Today I stood between this table and the window and I looked down at one of the pages that had drifted furthest from the place where I sit now writing about that page. I looked down and I saw on the page the words *my reader*. I read the two words, and then I thought of the man I was reading about.

I thought of that man reading the page I had been writing on when I got up from my table to walk to the window. I had been about to write on that page the name of a street in my native district. I had been about to write, before I wrote that name, that each name is more than one name. I had been about to write then that the name of a street in a district of Melbourne County might be also the name of a city one hundred and fifty kilometres north of that district. I was about to write next that the name of a city north of Melbourne County might also be the name of a town a hundred kilometres south-east of Ideal, South Dakota – the county seat of Rock County, Nebraska. I was going to write also that the name of a town in the grasslands of Nebraska might also be the name of a city in a book which is partly about a lilac tree and a row of tamarisk trees. And I was going to write, just before I wrote the name of the street in my native district, that the name of the city in the book that is partly about a lilac and a row of tamarisks is also the name of a city where I lived from my sixth year until my tenth year. And then I was going to write that when I was twelve years old and living in my native district I became interested in a girl who had only just arrived in my district and that I asked the girl what street she lived in and that she said she lived in Bassett Street.

I had been about to write what I have just written, but when I stood between my table and the window I thought for a moment what my reader would have thought if he had been reading the page where I had read the words *my reader*. I had thought for a moment what a man would think if he saw himself clearly named on a page he was reading.

I had thought of a man in a room very different from my room who had written the page that I was reading. I had thought of the man I had always thought of as my reader. I had thought of that man sitting at his table and not reading but writing. I had thought of him as having written all the pages around me. And then I thought of him as being about to write on the page that I had been about to write on when I left my table and walked towards the window. He was about to write on the page that I had been about to write on, except that he was going to write instead of the last words that I was going to write:

And then I was going to write that when I was twelve years old and living in my native district I became interested in a girl who had only just arrived in my district and that I asked the girl what street she lived in and that she said she lived in Bendigo Street.

In front of me on my table
is a clipping from a daily newspaper issued in the year
when I was eleven years old. The clipping comprises a
reproduction of a photograph together with a caption of
three lines underneath. At the centre of the photograph
the Catholic Archbishop of Melbourne County, the Most
Reverend Doctor Daniel Mannix, holds open a small book
and pretends to study the pages. Standing a little to one
side of the Archbishop are two schoolgirls of thirteen
or fourteen years. Each girl wears the pleated skirt and
blouse and tie and blazer and gloves and bowl-shaped hat
of the school uniform of Catholic colleges for girls in
Melbourne County thirty-five years ago. The book in the
outstretched hand of the Archbishop is rather far from

the eyes of the two schoolgirls, but the girls are polite and obedient; the photographer has told them to look at the pages of the book in the Archbishop's hand, and so they do. For the sake of appearances the two schoolgirls strain their white necks a little and compose their faces as though they are actually reading the pages held slightly beyond them.

On some nights in this room with books around the walls, I clear a space among these pages and I look at the newspaper photograph from thirty-five years ago. I look at the faces of the schoolgirls: at the clear skin of the faces and the alert and thoughtful eyes. On some nights in this room, after I have put aside my pages and after I have drunk my evening's beer, I promise myself I will take steps next day to insert in the same newspaper (which is still published in Melbourne County) a copy of the photograph (I assume the original is still in the archives of the newspaper) together with the names of the two girls and a request to each girl, as she was then, to write to me here in this room telling me simply where she lives and what name she uses nowadays, so that I can write to her at length and perhaps even send her some of these pages.

But the next morning in this room I put the clipping in a drawer and I do not take it out again until some night, months later, when I look at the photograph through a reading-glass trying to identify the monogram on each of the blazer pockets and so to learn which of the many colleges for Catholic girls in Melbourne County each of the two girls attended and which two streams she lived between in the years when I lived between the Moonee Ponds and the Merri.

In the photograph of thirty-five years ago the two girls are standing on one side while the Archbishop stands in the centre. The girls have been included in the photograph because they have been awarded prizes. They have won prizes in one of a group of competitions for children of all ages in Catholic schools of Melbourne County. The competitions have been conducted by a body called the Paraclete Arts Society.

The title *Paraclete* is used for the Holy Ghost, the third Person of the Blessed Trinity and traditionally the person of those three most ready to help writers, artists, and all who today would be called *creative*. I knew as a schoolboy in the early 1950s that the word *paraclete* was from the Greek and meant *helper*, or *comforter*, but I was struck then, as I am still struck today, by the likeness of the word *paraclete* to *parakeet*.

Almost certainly before I had heard the word *paraclete*, I had heard and learned the meaning of the word *parakeet*. And almost certainly before I had heard of a personage named the Holy Ghost who was one third of the God I was obliged to worship, I had become a worshipper of birds. I was never interested in the flight of birds – I have never watched the soaring of falcons or the gliding of gulls that writers about birds are so taken by. I have admired birds for as long as I can remember for their furtiveness.

Something else I knew as a schoolboy in the early 1950s was that I would have seemed foolish if I had revealed that I had a favourite among the Persons of the Trinity. Yet privately I much preferred the Holy Ghost to either the Father or the Son. Unlike the other two, the Holy Ghost was never represented in pictures as having a human shape. The Holy Ghost was shadowy and changeable. He was many things rather than one thing: sometimes a rushing wind and sometimes tongues of fire or a shaft of light. He was most often represented as a bird.

I am not writing about some milksop-child in a joke told by smiling nuns or priests. I knew the difference between the words *paraclete* and *parakeet*. But I knew already that each word is more than one word. And I was beginning to find messages and signs beneath the surfaces of words. I was struck by the roundabout ways of my thinking whenever I looked at a sketch of the bird that was meant to suggest the presence of the Holy Ghost and when I said aloud the word *paraclete* and heard at the same time the word *parakeet* and saw the gold collar and the grass-green and royal-blue body of *Barnardius barnardi*, Barnard's parakeet, or the ringneck parrot, close to the ground in the grasslands of the Mallee district far away past Mount Macedon.

I sometimes chose to see the two birds perched side by side: the dull-coloured, dove-shaped Paraclete and the vivid but furtive parakeet. The Paraclete was no less than the Third Person of the Triune God; the parakeet I recognise now as one of the demigods who live on earth rather than in heaven and who are all I know of divinity.

The Paraclete stood for the official religion, which seemed to me in those days a vast and not uninteresting body of doctrine that I might go on learning for the rest of my life. The parakeet stood for something that I knew was no part of the official religion, although I often wished it could have been: what I might have called the religion of grasslands. I could only have talked vaguely about the religion of grasslands. But whenever I stood alone in the paddocks near Sims Street, with Bendigo Street just in view over my shoulder, I felt without straining to feel it what I supposed I was meant to feel during prayers and ceremonies in church.

The two girls standing to one side of Archbishop Mannix have won first and second prize in the essay-writing section (for boys or girls under fourteen years at closing date) in the competitions conducted by the Paraclete Arts Society. Each girl has written an essay on the subject 'How I Can Help Newcomers From Europe To Be Good Catholics'. The girls have probably not yet seen a newcomer from Europe, but they know from their newspapers that several thousand people known as Balts will soon arrive in Melbourne County and that many more thousands of other Europeans are expected to follow the Balts.

Each year when the Paraclete Arts Society advertises its competitions, the nuns and the brothers in most of the

Catholic secondary schools of Melbourne County choose the few that they call their most talented pupils and compel them to enter. The boys or girls write drafts of their essays, which the nuns or brothers then edit and comment on. More drafts are written. These too are edited and even rewritten here and there by the teacher, but not to an extent that will prevent the same teacher later from certifying that the essay is the original and unaided work of the entrant in the competition. At last, on an afternoon when the rest of the school has gone home, the essay-writers sit in their strangely quiet classroom writing – with steel-nibbed pens and with blue Swan ink from a squat bottle instead of the black, gritty mixture of powder and water from the everyday inkwell. Each pupil has to write a faultless draft, in his or her best copperplate handwriting. From time to time the nun or the brother strides into the room and stands behind each pupil, silently checking the draft word by word. If the teacher finds an error, a finger points it out to the writer. A missing comma can be corrected by a stroke of the pen, but any other error obliges the pupil to abandon that page and to take a clean page and begin again.

I have never been able to identify the uniforms of the two prize-winning schoolgirls, but I have always supposed that those girls, like most of the prize-winning girls in my childhood, are from schools among the hills south of the Yarra Valley. On the night when she wrote her final draft, each girl stepped out onto a long veranda with archways between thick brick columns. She looked across the lawns and the gravel paths around her school to the wide shallow valley of the Yarra filling with mist; or she looked to the east, where the last sunlight picked out the few creases and folds in the forested mass of Mount Dandenong. Even if the girl had looked north-west she would have seen no further than the hills of Heidelberg. She could hardly have been curious to know that on the other side of those hills the flatlands began; that somewhere in that flatness the Merri flowed through its gorges; that further away still was the Moonee Ponds in its valley; that somewhere in the flat district between those two streams, on a slight hill marked by a few elm trees, was a building of timber and fibro-cement which on Sundays was the church of the parish of Blessed Oliver Plunket and on weekdays was the primary school of the same parish, and in one of the three rooms into which the building was divided on weekdays by sets of folding doors, seated alone at an oddly shaped piece of furniture which on Sundays served as a seat-and-kneeler in the church and on weekdays – folded somewhat differently – served as a desk in the classroom, was myself writing carefully the final draft of my essay 'How I Can Help Newcomers From Europe To Be Good Catholics'.

In the photograph I am standing beside Archbishop Mannix, on the opposite side from the two girls. I am not wearing any recognisable school uniform; I am wearing my best grey pullover and a white shirt with the top button undone. The photograph does not show my trousers, but they are short; that is, they reach from my waist to just above my knees. I am not wearing school uniform because my school has no uniform. Blessed Oliver Plunket's School is a parish primary school whereas the two girls are from secondary fee-paying schools, or what would be called today private schools.

The book with its pages open in the hands of the Archbishop is my prize. The two girls have finished first and second in the essay competition; my prize is for honourable mention. Yet because the girls are thirteen or fourteen and I am only eleven, and also because I am the only boy to have won any sort of prize that day in any of the different competitions for different ages in essay-writing, painting, or drawing – the only boy in my short trousers among all the pleated tunics and bowl-shaped hats and gloved hands and thick stockings; the only boy in my plain grey among all the fawns and browns and bottle-greens and sky-blues with crests and Latin mottoes on breast-pockets and thin stripes of two or three colours around necks and wrists and waists of pullovers – I have been chosen by the photographer from the morning newspaper to pose with Archbishop Mannix and the prize-winning girls.

All four of us – His Grace, the two girls, and myself – are looking with a show of interest at the book which is my prize. Anyone who glanced at the picture in the newspaper next morning and then read quickly through the caption would have found the picture quite unremarkable. But I have been looking at the picture each year for thirty-five years and learning a little more each year.

I am quite out of place in the picture. I am by far the smallest, and beside the aged face of Doctor Mannix and the pretty faces of the two girl-women my own face seems almost babyish. My short haircut exposes my jug-ears, and my child's forehead is absurdly knitted from the effort to appear solemn in the presence of my elders and betters. If I look at the clothing of the four people, I see the voluminous soutane and cape and the lofty biretta and pom-pom on the Archbishop, the elegant uniforms of the schoolgirls, and my own unbuttoned collar and kiddie's pullover – as though I have only just been called in to this formal gathering from playing in the sandpit outside.

Sometimes I look at the book that I am looking at in the hands of the Archbishop. Twenty years ago I used to suppose that the book was a book I had written myself. I had written every page of the book myself in an out-of-the-way place, and then I had left the book lying where it was sure to come under the notice of young women or girl-women. Two girl-women had found the book and had looked in its pages. Then they had brought the book and me, the writer of the book, to the Archbishop of Melbourne County. The girl-women had told the Archbishop that the book contained filth. They preferred to say no more – only that the book was full of filth.

Twenty years ago I used to see the two girl-women looking with stern faces at the book; the Archbishop first holding the book at arm's length and then turning a few pages gingerly; the Archbishop agreeing with the girl-women that the book was a vile book; myself being handed over to a room full of affronted girls for a summary trial and a humiliating punishment.

Ten years ago I still supposed that the book was a book I had written myself. The book was not vile or filthy, but its contents had still angered the girl-women. Once again they had brought me and my book before the Archbishop. But the venerable man was not interested in reading about grasslands and vast houses where silent young women stared out from library windows in the late afternoon. His Grace had stifled a dignified yawn and had given back the book to the girl-women, telling them the book contained nothing directly contrary to faith or morals. But that had not placated the girl-women. How, they asked one another, could this so-called prodigy with his naked knees and his clothes of plain grey – how could this child from the backlands in the north of their county dare to write about the dream-countries of elegant girl-women such as themselves? And then in the room filled with girl-women the fearsome sound of female tittering had broken out while I waited again for my sentence to be handed down.

On some nights in this room I think of rooms I will never see in the Institute of Prairie Studies and I wonder who has risen by now to become editor of *Hinterland*.

I used to fear the man in the archives surrounded by colour-plates of birds and relief-maps of plains, but the people I fear today are the women who were once the prize-winning schoolgirls.

The man with his colour-plates and relief-maps is no longer at the heart of the Institute of Prairie Studies. No footsteps sound today in the corridors leading past his suite of rooms. But the women who were once the prize-winning schoolgirls walk with short, firm steps across the red and the green of carpets between many offices with names of women on their doors. The skin of the women is still clear and their eyes are still wide. The women would still consent today to look at the opened pages of a book in order to oblige a photographer, although they would not consent to stand beside a shabby stranger.

Seated at their desks each morning, the women read the first of the latest letters to have reached them. Then the women prepare their replies – not by writing with pens on paper but by pressing with their fingers on buttons or by speaking to their secretaries in other rooms. The women tell their secretaries what to write in reply to the latest of many letters that begin by explaining that the writer of the letter has kept for many years a certain clipping from a newspaper.

When the women have told the young women their secretaries what words to write in reply to all the writers of letters, then the main business of the day begins. The women go on with their task of preparing the contents of *Hinterland*. They touch rows of buttons on quiet machines and they look into panes of clouded glass.

In my thinking I tread softly past the offices with the names of women on the doors. Many years ago I got up from my game of arranging glass marbles in the dust. I got up and washed my hands and knees and sat down at a desk and wrote as the nun my teacher suggested. My parroted words were read by a society of people who wanted the Holy Ghost to live in the hearts of writers and painters. When the society of people had seen that my words were as well-parroted as the words of girl-women two or three years older than me, then I was invited by the society into a room filled with many-coloured school uniforms and with calm female faces staring out from under bowl-shaped hats. In that room the many girl-women ceased their murmuring and watched while I walked forward boldly with my baby-face and my pink, scrubbed knees and while I accepted with no surprise or nervousness the book that was presented to me as my reward for having out-parroted so many girls and girl-women.

I still have the newspaper clipping to remind me of what a parroter I was, but in my thinking today about *Hinterland* and the Calvin O. Dahlberg Institute, I step softly across the red and the green and past the offices where the women look into their panes of glass. I step softly on my way to the depths of the building with many rooms and many windows – to the room where my reader reads that *Barnardius barnardi* is most often seen close to the ground and among grasses.

On the day when the first north wind made me think of the colours of the fish pond, I thought also of the girl from Bendigo Street but I was afraid I would not see her again after the school year had ended and the summer holidays had begun. Each of us was going to leave the school where we had sat all year in the same classroom. Before the coming summer had ended, we would be travelling away from our district in different directions each morning, each of us dressed in the uniform of a Catholic secondary school.

In my backyard, from the time when the leaves of the fig-tree had come forth, I had been preparing for the summer. I was afraid that the girl from Bendigo Street would be noticed by boys older and taller than myself when she travelled by tram or train away from our district.

The girl and I were almost the same age – a few months younger than thirteen years. I was still in short trousers. She was thin and flat-chested. I sensed that her body would soon grow, as some bodies had already grown among the girls in our class. I was not afraid that this would change things between us, but I was afraid that some boy-man two or three years older than myself would notice the growing body and would mutter a few words to her with the easy authority of such boy-men and would compel the girl-woman from Bendigo Street to go off with him and to forget me.

When I tried to see myself in future walking around my native district and knowing that a certain girl-woman still lived in Bendigo Street but that some boy-man or some young man had power over her, I saw my native district drained of colour like the newspaper photographs of grey, ruined places in Europe after the war.

Someone reading this page deep in the Institute of Prairie Studies may wonder why a man of my age and standing writes at this table for day after day about a twelve-years-old child. But I am not writing about a twelve-years-old child. Each person is more than one person. I am writing about a man who sits at a table in a room with books around the wall and who writes for day after day with a heaviness pressing on him.

The girl from Bendigo Street was not a native of the district between the Moonee Ponds and the Merri. She had been born a few kilometres to the south, among the loops and wanderings of the Yarra as it approaches the sea. The girl and her parents had come to live in my district early in the year when we were both twelve. They had come from East Melbourne, which at that time was a district of rooming houses and shabby rented cottages and what the writers for newspapers called underworld haunts. One of the ways that the girl found for annoying me was to talk about what she called her old gang in East Melbourne: how they had played together all through the weekends and late on summer evenings on strips of lawn in the middle of streets or in the corners of a small park.

The girl would tell me she was homesick for her native district, and I would try to look indifferent while I thought of some gangster's son kissing her among the bushes of East Melbourne.

Two or three couples among the older children at my school were widely known to be boyfriend and girlfriend, and few children had commented when I let it be known soon after the girl from Bendigo Street had arrived at my school that I considered her my girlfriend. The girl herself tried to appear indifferent to me or even annoyed with me in public. I believed I understood her, and I tried not to force my company on her, and every few days she rewarded me by telling me quietly something that was unimportant in itself but seemed a message from beneath the surface of her. Away from school we were more easy with one another. If I walked my dog Belle along Bendigo Street on a Sunday afternoon, and if I loitered near the girl's house until her dog began to bark in the backyard, the girl would nearly always come out through the front door. She would step into her black rubber boots that had been standing beside the doormat. Then she would walk to her front gate and talk with me for a few minutes agreeably, and even a little shyly.

That was how things stood between myself and the girl from Bendigo Street for the first six months after we had met. I called her my girlfriend and she sometimes spoke warmly to me. She was clever with words, although probably not as clever as I was. Yet I did not try to impress her with words. I had never thought to tell her of how I had won a prize for an essay in the year before she had arrived in my district. I could only think of impressing her by some feat at football or cricket or running, none of which I was clever at. I did not know in those days that young men sometimes performed feats with words in the hope of impressing young women.

That was how things stood between us until a certain day of heavy rain six months after I had first met the girl from Bendigo Street. The day of rain was one of the last days of winter according to the newspapers of Melbourne County. The same day was about half-way through the season after Pentecost according to the calendar of the Church.

Late in the afternoon of the rainy day our classroom was for some reason half-empty and our teacher was not with us. The girl from Bendigo Street was sitting with one of her girlfriends just behind the desk where I was sitting alone. Somehow the girl from Bendigo Street and I began the game of talking to the other girl as though she was carrying messages between us and as though we two were out of earshot of one another. The girl from Bendigo Street might have told the girl in the middle to tell me that she, the girl from Bendigo Street, was sick to death of me hanging around her in the schoolyard. I might then have told the girl in the middle to tell the girl from Bendigo Street that I was fed up with her stories of the gang of slum kids in East Melbourne.

The girl in the middle was herself new to the school, but I had known her three years before at another school in another district. That other school too had elm trees near by, and when I lived in that other district I had not wanted to leave it.

I have written already in these pages that I do not read the books on the shelves around me. I do not read the books nowadays but I read a few of the books when I was younger, and even today I still sometimes handle some of the books and I sometimes glance into the pages of some book that I read many years ago.

I keep mostly to this room. I am in this room every day, writing at this table with shelves of books on all the walls around me. I look up often at the books on their shelves. Sometimes I look at the words on the spines of the books, but mostly I look at the colours on the spines.

I find patterns when I look at the spines of two or more books together. Every day I notice for the first time a pattern in the spines of certain books. And every day the new pattern is a little wider than the patterns that I noticed on earlier days.

Last year, or it may have been another year, I used to admire such a pattern as three or four adjacent spines of white, red, white, red, or the like. Later I may have noticed that a similar pattern I had also admired on the shelf above could be seen as linked with the first simple pattern in a larger pattern if I could have recognised a half-dozen spines of dark green between the two simple clusters and if I could have recognised also a dark green at an outer corner of the newly forming pattern and perhaps another dark green at another corner as all belonging together. Now, in these days when I mostly keep to this room, my eye has learned to make out patterns reaching across three or four shelves and for as wide as my outstretched arms, and patterns of not just the obvious colours such as red, white, and green, but grey and gold and lilac and brown. And lately I have included in some of the wider patterns shades and variants of the first colours that I noticed: of the red and the white and the green.

Someone reading this page may expect me to write that I believe every colour of every spine on every shelf in this room is part of a pattern, and that I hope to recognise the pattern in time. I have to remind that reader, if such a reader exists, that this room has four walls and that every wall has shelves of books somewhere on it, which means that the room has no vantage-point from where I could stare at all the shelves together. I have sometimes thought of learning by heart the colour of every spine on every book in this room and of sitting here with my eyes closed and dreaming of myself seeing all four walls as one large wall in front of me. I believe I could memorise the colours and the exact positions of even more books than I see here in this room; but I cannot believe I could dream of seeing all those books at once and in one pattern. Faced with so many colours, I would need to have a few pages like these pages in front of me and a pen in my hand and my eyes open in order to write the few words needed to keep in front of my eyes the one wall and the one pattern. And if I must have pages and a pen, then I must have a table to rest them on. But a table and a chair for sitting at the table would have to be surrounded by a room, and a room has to have walls, and I cannot think of walls around me unless those walls have books somewhere on them. And so, in order to understand the pattern in this room I would have to sit in another room with other books on the walls around me. And in that other room I could not stop myself from trying to make out patterns and then larger patterns and then wanting to see all four walls as one wall where one pattern appeared. But in order to dream of that one wall, I would have to sit in another room.

I do not read books nowadays but I sometimes handle books and sometimes I even look into a book. If the book is a book that I read long ago, I look at a few pages. But if the book is one of the many that I have never read, I read the words on the dust-jacket and in the preliminary pages. I am not so stupid that I suppose the words I read are telling me about the other pages – the pages of the text that I will never read. I suppose instead that the words I read at the front and the back of the book and even the illustrations and the patterns on the dust-jacket are telling me about the pages of text in some other book. The other book is nowhere on my shelves. I may never see the other book. I cannot guess what colours might be on the dust-jacket of that other book, or what words at its front and its back might tell about the inner pages of some other book still.

Or the other pages – the pages of the text that I only read about – are between the covers of no other book. Those pages have drifted away who knows where. Sometimes I think of all the drifting pages of the world as having been collected and brought together in buildings of many rooms in grassy landscapes under skies filled with clouds, and as having been bound, after all their drifting, into dream-books with dream-patterns on their jackets and dream-colours on their spines and dream-words on their preliminary pages, and as having been stored on the shelves of a dream-library.

Yet sometimes a drifting page drifts away from the drifting pages around it. Such a page might drift in among other sorts of pages – even in among the preliminary pages of books such as these books around me here.

One day in this room I read in the preliminary pages of an unlikely book these words:

There is another world but it is in this one.
Paul Eluard

I cannot remember having read the inner pages of the book in whose outer pages I found these words. I have never taken the trouble to find out who Paul Eluard is or was. I prefer to think of who he might have been: a man whose life's work was to compose, perhaps in some language other than my own, a sentence that has drifted far away from the pages where it was first written and has come to rest for the time being in one of the preliminary pages of a book in this room where I sometimes get up from my table in order to open the front pages of some book whose spine has made me dream of myself reading the pages that must have drifted long before into some dream-book.

There is another world, and I have seen parts of that world on most days of my life. But the parts of that world are drifting past and cannot be lived in. For as long as I used to see drifting past me those parts of the other world, I used to wonder about the place where all the drifting parts drifted together. But I no longer wondered after I had read the words attached to the name Paul Eluard.

There is another world but it is in this one...So say the words printed among the preliminary pages of one of the books that I have never read. But what place exactly do the words *this one* refer to? They cannot refer to the space between the covers of the book where I found them. I have never yet found a book whose preliminary pages and whose inner pages belong together. And in any case, the name of the author on the front of my book is not Paul Eluard but Patrick White. The words *this one* can only refer to the so-called world between the covers of a book I have never seen: a book whose author is a man named Paul Eluard.

Perhaps those words from Paul Eluard first appeared in the preliminary pages of a book of his. But I repeat: I have never found any book whose preliminary pages belonged with its inner pages, which means that the other world is within drifting pages that I will almost certainly never see: pages in a dream-book that I can only dream of.

On the other hand, the words of Paul Eluard might have first appeared on the inner pages of one of his books. In that case, I have to understand the words somewhat differently. If the words were in the inner pages of a book, they can only have been uttered by a narrator or a character – by one of those people who inhabit the inner pages of books. There is another world, says one of those people deep inside the pages of a book, but it is in – and therefore at one remove further from you out there – this world where I am now.

The other world, in other words, is a place that can only be seen or dreamed of by those people known to us as narrators of books or characters within books. If you or I, reader, happen to glimpse part of that world drifting past, as it were, it is because we have seen or dreamed of ourselves seeing for a moment as a narrator or a character in a book sees or dreams of seeing.

If someone reading this page is thinking of Paul Eluard as a living man uttering his words in the place that is usually called the real world and referring perhaps to something as simple as a world he has dreamed of or the world in which the characters in books lead their so-called lives, then I can only answer that if a man named Paul Eluard walked into this room tonight and uttered his mysterious words, I would understand Mr Eluard as my reader wants to understand him. But until Paul Eluard comes into my room I have only a copy of his written words. He wrote his words and at the instant of his writing them the words entered the world of narrators and characters and landscapes – not to mention pages that drift into other books where they might be read by people such as myself.

But what if Paul Eluard wrote no book? What if the only words he wrote in all his life are the ten mysterious words, which he wrote only once on a blank page before setting the page adrift? *There is another world but it is in this one*...Even then, the words are still written. However, in this case the other world must be understood as lying within the virgin whiteness which is all that part of the page where, as yet, no word has been written.

In desks one in front of the other, in the senior classroom of the Catholic primary school on a low hilltop east of the valley of the Moonee Ponds, while a wind drove rain-clouds from the grasslands west of Melbourne County over my native district, I sat with the girl from Bendigo Street and a girl from Bendigo.

The girl from Bendigo Street had arrived in my district from East Melbourne in the first week of February. Two weeks later a family that included three children had arrived

in my district from the city of Bendigo, and the girl from
that family had come to sit in the class that included myself
and the girl from Bendigo Street.

Even if I had not already chosen the girl from Bendigo
Street, I would not have been interested in the girl from
Bendigo as a girlfriend. But I looked into her face on every
hot afternoon in the last weeks of that summer. And while
I looked into her face I looked from the sides of my eyes
at the tops of the elm trees in Raeburn Reserve.

Three years before, the girl from Bendigo had sat near
me in a classroom from the windows of which I had seen
the tops of a row of elm trees in McCrae Street, Bendigo.
In the same year, on hot afternoons in December, the
girl and I had been among the children who walked in
file beneath the elm trees in Rosalind Park on our way to
practise for our Christmas concert in the Capitol Theatre
in View Street. In the classroom in my native district I was
enjoying what has been the chief pleasure of my life, which
is to see two places I had thought far apart lying in fact
in one place – not simply adjoining one another but each
appearing to enclose or even to embody the other.

I had lived in the district between Bendigo Creek and
Huntly Race for longer than I had lived anywhere during
my childhood. I had thought while I lived there that the
district between Bendigo Creek and Huntly Race would
be for me what a native district is for many other people.
But I had been taken away from that district and from the
city of Bendigo when I was nine years old, and I had not

seen those places since. Before the girl from Bendigo had arrived in my native district I had sometimes looked at the elm trees in Raeburn Reserve, but while I looked I had not thought I was looking at some part of the city of Bendigo. Yet when I looked at the face of the girl from Bendigo in my classroom so that I saw the elm trees in Raeburn Reserve only from the sides of my eyes, then I saw that the elm trees were the trees of McCrae Street, Bendigo. And I even saw, without taking my eyes away from the face of the girl from Bendigo, the elm trees further along McCrae Street towards the corner of Baxter Street, and the elm trees around the corner in Baxter Street where I would walk that afternoon on my way from my school to my home in the district between Bendigo Creek and Huntly Race.

Perhaps someone reading this page believes I should not have written that a family with three children moved from a district of Bendigo to the one district of all the districts of Melbourne County where a boy who often remembered a city named Bendigo had chosen for his girlfriend a girl who lived in a street named Bendigo. That reader would probably believe also that I should not write that the girl from Bendigo became friendly with the girl from Bendigo Street, so much so that on a day of heavy rain when the classroom happened to be almost empty and the children in the room were free to sit where they pleased, the girl from Bendigo Street sat with the girl from Bendigo while I sat near both of them, turning often to say to the girl from Bendigo what I wanted to say to the girl from Bendigo Street and what the girl from Bendigo Street could hear clearly although she kept her head down and showed no sign of having heard.

Anyone who believes I should not have written what I have written does not understand what a man named Eluard once wrote on the inner pages of a book or on an otherwise blank page that he later set adrift. Such a reader does not understand that each place has another place within it.

Such a reader does not trust the words of the man named Eluard as I trust them. And I trust the words to this extent: that if it were not by definition impossible for me to tell my reader where I am at this moment, I would write on this page that I am at this moment in another world but that the world where I am is in this one.

Each of us – the girl from Bendigo Street and myself – told the other through the girl from Bendigo all the faults we had found in one another: all our reasons for disliking one another. Each of us spoke just loudly enough for the other to hear the words above the murmuring of the few children in the room and the beating of the rain against the windows. And although the girl from Bendigo knew that the girl from Bendigo Street and I heard one another, she acted faithfully as our go-between and passed on our messages as though we were far apart.

We hardly looked at one another. The girl from

Bendigo Street kept her head down over her schoolbook and I looked mostly at the rain and the grey sky. I saw the yellow of her hair only from the sides of my eyes.

Our game of complaining against one another did not seem tedious to me. It seemed a game of almost boundless promise. The more we found fault with one another and pressed down on the one side of the balance, the more we seemed to promise one another that a heavy counter-weight would later be placed on the other side.

The girl from Bendigo Street guided me towards the end of our game. She suggested to me – still through the girl from Bendigo – that I who found so many faults in her would surely find fault with most other girls.

I saw where she was leading me. I told her that I did find fault with most girls.

In that case, it was suggested to me, I would surely not have chosen a girlfriend for myself.

She could believe me or not, she was told, but I had chosen a girlfriend six months before.

So we went on. My girlfriend would have been this sort of person or that sort. She would have lived far away in this or that place. She had surely never set foot in the district between the Moonee Ponds and the Merri...

Our game still seemed endlessly promising. We might have gone on playing it for day after day, I thought. I might have talked about fanciful versions of myself, each with a girlfriend in a district far from my native district, and I might have said about those fanciful people what

155

I could never have said about myself and the girl I was talking to.

But the girl from Bendigo Street asked in good time the question whose answer she could hardly have doubted. And writing this today I admire her sense of decorum. Of the two words commonly used by children at our school when they talked about girlfriends and boyfriends, she chose not the word from the hit parade songs that we both knew well: not the word that belonged with outlines of hearts pierced by arrows. She chose instead the more discreet word. She chose the word that we might have used to one another's face without being embarrassed and without feeling as though we were only children playing at being adults.

I had told the girl from Bendigo Street through the girl from Bendigo that my girlfriend in fact lived between the Moonee Ponds and the Merri. The question was then put to me: if I liked a girl from that district, who did I like?

I wonder whether or not I spoke my answer. I wonder whether I said to the girl from Bendigo the words *I like her*. And I wonder whether I stressed the last of those three words heavily and whether I stared while I spoke the words at the bowed head of the girl from Bendigo Street so that she could hear fully the sound of every letter of every word.

I cannot remember. I suspect that I simply pointed at the bowed head and that the girl from Bendigo then whispered my meaning to the girl from Bendigo Street, in which case the girl from Bendigo Street did not hear the sound of my voice. I suspect I had begun to feel already the arrogance that came over me many years later on the very few occasions when I seemed to have another person in my power. But if I simply pointed my finger, and if my pointing was in any way arrogant, yet I can remember at least that the head with the yellow hair remained bowed: the girl from Bendigo Street could not have seen me.

If I did not speak – and if the girl from Bendigo Street did not hear me say what I felt towards her on that rainy afternoon nearly forty years ago – then I offer to that girl the words I am about to write on this page.

Even if I had spoken to the girl from Bendigo in the hearing of the girl from Bendigo Street, I would have used the more cautious word – the word that the girl from Bendigo Street, with her faultless girl-woman's tact, had put in my way. I would have said *I like her*. But by now enough time has passed, I think, for me to use the bolder word. Today I write *I love her*.

The words I have just written are written as though to a go-between. But a man who writes on pages such as these can only have for his go-between his reader. If I could think of my reader as a man or a woman in a room with a window looking towards Mount Macedon across the last traces of the grasslands north of Melbourne County, then I could suppose at least that my message will fall into the hands of someone who remembers the district between the Moonee Ponds and the Merri as it was in the early years of the 1950s and remembers a street named Bendigo where the water lay in long puddles all through the winter and remembers a girl who lived in that street.

But anyone who writes on pages such as these can only have for his reader someone in the Calvin O. Dahlberg Institute – and not even some woman who touches rows of buttons and who stares into cloudy glass, but some man like the writer himself: a man among the least-frequented corridors and in one of the least-visited rooms.

In her own message to me the girl from Bendigo Street outdid me. After I had spoken or nodded or pointed, I had turned to the window and waited for an answer. I was not uneasy. In the months while we had known one another the girl from Bendigo Street had been teaching me – whether she knew it or not – the language of girl-women, and well before the rainy afternoon I had translated some of what she had told me into my own language.

The answer came to me promptly. The girl from Bendigo looked at me and said the words *She says she likes you very much.*

I was only a child of not quite thirteen years who thought he knew as much and felt as strongly as any boy or girl of his age in any country of the world, but I heard in the sound of the last two words spoken by the girl from Bendigo something that surprised me. It was something that the girl from Bendigo too must have heard in the sound of the same two words when the girl from Bendigo Street had spoken them to her so softly that I had not heard any words from where I was sitting. The girl from Bendigo had spoken the first five of her words softly and then she had paused for part of a moment. She had paused for just long enough so that whenever I have dreamed of myself hearing her words since that day, I have heard as clearly as though it was a word itself the silence that came before her last two words.

When I hear the silence that comes between my own words sometimes, I think of prairies or plains – as though all my words are being spoken from grasslands. But whenever I hear the silence that comes between the first five and the last two of the seven words spoken to me by the girl from Bendigo, I think of depths.

I did not hear the words whispered by the girl from Bendigo Street, but I understand that they must have comprised a sentence with a main clause whose verb was in the imperative mood followed by a noun clause whose verb was a part of the verb *to like* in the present tense, indicative mood. If such a sentence was spoken to me, and if I obeyed the command in the main clause, I would report to the person denoted by the pronoun which was the object of the verb in the main clause a sentence beginning with a main clause whose verb was in the past historic tense. If I had been the girl from Bendigo on that rainy afternoon I would have used the past historic tense of the verb *to say* in the sentence that I spoke to the boy who was myself on that day. But my writing this only shows how little I know of the language of girl-women. The girl from Bendigo understood perfectly the words of the girl from Bendigo Street. The girl from Bendigo reported all that was stated and implied in the words that she heard from the girl from Bendigo Street. Those words were in the language of girl-women, and that language includes a tense which appears identical to the present tense in my language but which denotes an action that can never have been brought to an end.

At some time during the years after that rainy afternoon, a new church and a new school, each of brick, were built in the paddock next to the church-school where I sat with the girl from Bendigo and the girl from Bendigo Street. The old building was later destroyed by fire, if I have remembered accurately something that one of my brothers wrote to me in a letter. Whenever I have written about the building that I knew on the slight hill in Landells Road, I have used the past historic tense: the simple tense prescribed by my language for actions completed in the past. But whenever I have thought of writing a sentence with verbs of that tense to report the words spoken to me by the girl from Bendigo, which words in turn were to report to me the words whispered by the girl from Bendigo Street, I have been unable to translate the verbs used by either girl from their original tense in the language of girl-women. I have never been able to write that the actions denoted by the whispered verbs have been brought to an end. Much else has been brought to an end, but those words remain untranslatable.

In the spring of the year when I was twelve, in the last weeks of the season after Pentecost, whenever the afternoon was warm I leaned against the lower branches of a fig-tree and prepared myself for the end of the summer that had not even begun.

Four months from then, in the hot days of February, I would have been wearing the uniform of a boys' secondary school and travelling each day to my new school by tram. At the same time my girlfriend, the girl from Bendigo Street, would have put on the uniform of a girls' secondary school and would have begun, too, to travel – but on a different tram. We would no longer see each other every day. For most of the week we would be in opposite corners of our district. And yet our lives would be more crowded than before with events that we wanted to describe to one another.

I had planned easily how my girlfriend and I would meet one another four or five years from then, when we were old enough to go together on the evening bus to the cinemas in the main street of our district. I had planned even more easily that we would marry four or five years afterwards and live in a large house on the other side of Mount Macedon where I would train racehorses and she would breed pedigreed golden cocker spaniels. But all I could devise for us in the summer to come was her calling at my house sometimes on her way from the tram terminus to her own home. She would call at my house to pat my dog Belle, who met her own dog sometimes when I walked with Belle along Sims Street at the edge of the grasslands. Or the girl from Bendigo Street would call at my own house sometimes to sit beside the fish pond.

Without the fish pond, I thought, I could not have invited my girlfriend to my home. It would have seemed a drab invitation to a girl-woman to ask her into an unremarkable backyard. But the pond distinguished my backyard; and when my girlfriend and I sat beside the pond – even if we sat on the wired-together wooden chairs from my kitchen and drank cordial and water from the glasses that had once held cheese spread or lemon butter – the pond would have made us feel older and more elegant.

The grass around the base of the pond would be long and unkempt, I hoped, when my girlfriend first called. While we talked she would glance at the pond and at the lawn around it; she would be enjoying the illusion that the pond did not rest on the ground: that the rows of bricks reached far below the level of our feet and therefore that the clouded green water was far deeper than she had first supposed – perhaps too deep for her to touch the bottom, even if she leaned far over the wall.

But she would never reach her hand so far into the water. She would be like myself in preferring many possible things to any one visible thing. Besides, she would be wearing her new school uniform, and even in the hot days of February a jacket with a long-sleeved shirt or blouse underneath. She would not reach her hand into the water, but she would sit in a ladylike way on the wall of bricks. She would sit there in her pale brown or sky-blue and I would stand beside her – in long trousers at last: long, dark-grey trousers. She would sit and I would stand. We would be quite still. We would be waiting for the fish to drift into view.

I would have told her well beforehand how timid the fish were. If she moved abruptly or even if she spoke too loudly the fish would go back into the depths again. But if she was quiet and patient a fish would appear; she would see the blunt red body and the long fluent tail.

In time she would grow used to the fish pond; she would notice it less. She and I would still sit beside the pond but we would talk like a brother and a sister who had been together for as long as they could remember. One afternoon she would notice a streak of red at the side of the shed. The leaves of the grapevine would be turning red. Then the afternoons would turn cool and misty, but by that time we would be so easy together that she could sit with me in the front room that was kept tidy for my parents' few visitors.

In time we might hardly look at the fish pond, but I could always think of the column of green going down into the ground. I could always think of the shaft of green water. Nor would the girl forget the pond. On many a day while she travelled between Bendigo Street and her school in the far corner of our district, some young man much older than myself would begin to talk to her. My girlfriend would answer politely but coldly. She would be thinking of the pond.

Our pond would not be the only secret sign between the girl from Bendigo Street and myself. In the years between our leaving school and our marrying, I would turn my father's fowl sheds into an aviary. I would begin to collect the birds that would live and breed in aviaries around our house in all the years when the girl from Bendigo Street and I lived on the other side of Mount Macedon. Even before I bought my first birds I would have planted shrubs and long-stemmed grasses inside the wire-mesh walls. The aviary would become a much bolder sign than the pond: a column of rich green rising out of the bare soil of the fowl yard. Inside the green the parrots and finches and ground-dwelling birds would thrive out of sight.

The wide district between Scotchman's Creek and Elster Creek is on the opposite side of Melbourne County from the district between the Moonee Ponds and the Merri. The soil of that wide district is mostly sandy, with swamps and heaths and tea-tree scrub instead of grasslands.

I lived between Scotchman's Creek and the Elster, in my parents' house, from the year when I was thirteen until the year when I was twenty. Those were the years when I learned to keep to my room, as I keep to this room today, and when I began to write on pages like these pages in front of me today. In those years also I forgot what little I had already learned of the language of girl-women, and I did not learn anything of the language of young women.

Each day in those years I rested for an hour or two from my writing on pages, and I left my room and walked among the streets of the district. While I walked I watched girl-women and young women, but without approaching them or speaking to them. After I had lived for a few years in the district I knew perhaps a hundred girl-women and young women by their faces and by the houses where they lived and sometimes by the shops or the factories where they worked or the schools they attended, but I knew none of their names and I had not spoken to any of them.

When I was twenty years old I prepared to leave the district between Scotchman's Creek and the Elster. I still wrote often on pages like this page but I was not so contented with keeping to my room. And I was not so contented with watching girl-women and young women but not being able to speak their language. I had decided to live in another district of Melbourne County where the language of females might be easier to learn.

Even though I was by then much more a young man than a boy-man, I watched many more girl-women than young women. By then the language of females had come to seem so strange to me that I thought I could only begin to learn that language if I heard it spoken simply at first by a girl-woman.

One morning I saw in a newspaper a photograph of one of the girl-women I had sometimes watched. I had watched her in the low hills south of the valley of Scotchman's Creek, and I knew the street she lived in, which was on the side of one of those hills. One day the girl-woman had looked almost into my face when I passed her in the street, and I had thought I understood her look, although I seldom understood the looks of females.

Underneath the photograph was the girl-woman's name, which I had not known before. I have already written that name on a few of these pages.

From the text around the photograph I learned that the age of the girl-woman was fourteen and that she was in the second form at her secondary school and that her teachers thought well of her. I learned that her family consisted of her mother and herself and that the mother and the daughter were what had been called in earlier years newcomers from Europe. I learned that the girl-woman, like myself, kept often to her room. And I also learned that she liked to sleep with her window open.

What I had learned from the newspaper might have been almost enough to prompt me to speak to the girl-woman if we had happened to meet in the street near her house when I was walking past in the days after I had read about her.

But what I had mainly learned was that the girl-woman and I would never happen to meet in the street again. On the night before I had seen her photograph and learned her name, the girl-woman had been in her bed in her room with the window open. Someone had climbed in through the open window and had used a hammer or a small axe to break the girl's skull and to kill her. I learned last of all from the newspaper that the police had not learned who might have climbed in through the window of the room.

I decided never to walk again in the streets between Scotchman's Creek and Elster Creek, even though I had never walked by night and I had never once spoken to any of the girl-women or the young women I had seen on my walks.

During the following days I thought often about the dead girl-woman. I hoped she had been asleep when the hammer or the small axe had first hit her, and that she had died at once. But then I read in a weekly newspaper that she had been hit many times and that she had struggled while she was being hit.

I next learned that the police had charged a man with having murdered the girl-woman. The man was as old then, when I was twenty, as I was ten years ago. His address was the same as the address of the dead girl-woman and her mother. His surname was different from theirs, but it was a name from the same part of the world as theirs.

Even after the man had been charged with the murder, I took no more walks in the district between Scotchman's Creek and Elster Creek, and I looked at no more girl-women or young women between those streams. I had already left that district and left my parents' house, and I was living in a rented room nearer to my native district when I read the newspaper reports of the trial of the man who was said to have killed the girl-woman.

The man was what was called in those days the *de facto*

husband of the mother of the girl-woman. Some months before the killing of the girl-woman, so it was said, the man had begun the practice of leaving the house by the front door nearly every night at about nine o'clock. He would tell the mother of the girl-woman that he was going to visit a man for an hour. He had not visited any man, so it was said, but had gone to the side of the house and had climbed through the open window of the girl's room and had spent the hour with her.

In time, so it was said, the girl-woman had learned that she was carrying a child and she had told this to the man. A few nights afterwards, so it was said, the man had climbed in through the window with a hammer. The man had brought the hammer down on the girl-woman's head while she lay awake in bed but he had not killed her at first. The girl had struggled but the man had gone on hitting her until she was dead. She had not cried out while she struggled.

The members of the jury believed all that was said against the man. But several times during the trial of the man the mother of the dead girl-woman had cried out that the things being said had not in fact happened. Sometimes the mother of the dead girl-woman had cried out in the language most commonly spoken in Melbourne County, but sometimes she had cried out in the heavy-hearted language of her own part of the world.

Each night when I get up from this table, I leave my pages lying wherever they happen to lie. I walk away from this table and I do not look at my pages again until the following afternoon.

I do not look at my pages until afternoon, but I arrive in this room long before midday and I stand for a long time in front of the windows or in front of the spines of books before I look at the pages on the table. And long before I look at the pages on the table, I watch the pages from the sides of my eyes.

I have found a way of watching a thing that shows me what I never see when I look at the thing. If I watch a thing from the sides of my eyes, I see in the thing the shape of another thing.

What I see when I watch from the sides of my eyes is the thing I would see if I stood a little way off, in a place where I can never stand for as long as I stand where I am standing. Or what I see when I watch from the sides of my eyes is what another man would see if he looked from a place a little to one side of me.

Watching from the sides of my eyes I see a shaft of greenish water rising out of the grass of fields. When I turn and look through my windows I see a row of poplar trees. A man standing a little to the side of me looks through the window in the usual way and sees a column of greenish water.

On some afternoons I look through the windows in the usual way and I see a long pole pointing at the sky. But a man standing a little to the side of me sees the shape of another thing reaching out from the land.

On some mornings when I stand for a long time in this room but without looking at all the pages strewn on the table, I watch the pages from the sides of my eyes. I see among the scattered pages the shapes of white or grey clouds. Afterwards, when I walk to my table and stand in front of my pages, I see only my scattered pages; but another man standing a little to one side of me might see clouds white or grey whenever he looks at my table.

The man a little to one side of me might suppose I am writing on clouds. He might even suppose that the clouds that he sees on my table are drifting away towards the clouds in the sky on the other side of my windows, or towards the clouds in the panes of glass in front of my books, or even towards the clouds on the other side of the spines and the covers of my books and other books.

Yet I have not forgotten that I once wrote on one of these pages that I was going to send the pages to a young woman who was dreaming of herself at a desk with printed pages around her and on top of each page the word *Hinterland* and somewhere among the first of the printed pages a sentence declaring her to be the editor of all those pages.

I have written already, on a page among these heaps of pages, that the men and women whose names are on the pages of books, or even on the spines and covers of books, are all dead. And I have written already, on a page among these heaps of pages, that the pages I am writing on are not the pages of books. But if these pages of mine drift away from this table, and if the pages drift in among the pages that drift like clouds in the space like sky behind all the rooms like these with books around the walls, then someone in future may find one of these pages drifting and may take it for a page of a book.

Anyone finding one of these pages and taking it for a page of a book might suppose that the people named on the page are dead. I have kept my own name well away from these pages, but anyone finding a page in future may suppose that Gunnarsen or his wife or anyone else named in these pages as a living person – that any such person died at some time while I was here at my table writing about such persons. Anyone finding even this page in future may suppose that the people I once dreamed of myself seeing in the Calvin O. Dahlberg Institute of Prairie Studies – that those people are dead who sometimes thought of me as dead, while I am still alive.

Today I thought of people who are already dead or who will soon die.

I do not say today that I have never looked behind the covers or the spine of any book, but I would have said this morning that I could not remember when I last turned the key in any of the glass doors in front of my shelves. This morning I turned a key and swung a pair of glass doors apart and then back against the shelves. I looked up and saw the spines of books with no images of sky or clouds among them.

I had decided to glance into the space behind the covers of books. I had decided to look at the sorts of words that are written about people who have died or who are supposed to have died. I was looking for words such as the man would see who stands a little to one side of me – the man who sees these pages as drifting and who supposes I have died.

Many years ago I saw in a book a few words in praise of Thomas Hardy as having been the first writer of books to write about the sound of the wind in tiny, bell-shaped heath flowers. But I neglected at the time to look for the book with the words describing the sound of the wind, and I neglected even to write the name of the book. Later, I forgot the name of the book in which I had first seen the words about the sound of the wind in the heath-flowers in the pages of a certain book by Thomas Hardy.

Today I remembered a mention of wind among grass and flowers in the last paragraph of *Wuthering Heights*, by Emily Brontë. I have read that book three times: first in 1956, then in 1967, and then again in 1977. I have read the book only three times in the past thirty years, but I am reading it more frequently – as the dates above show. The dates above remind me also that I have to read *Wuthering Heights* again before 1986 has ended. And I should write here also that on most of the days in the past thirty years when I have not been reading *Wuthering Heights* I have stared at the spine of it or at a corner of the cover of it. I have stared, and I have dreamed of myself seeing a boy-man and a girl-woman and grasslands.

I got up from my table today and took down the book from its shelf and turned to the last paragraph and read it aloud. The paragraph is all one sentence, and a memorable sentence, and while I read it aloud I dreamed of myself seeing headstones of graves with grass-stems swaying near by and clusters of tiny flower-heads among the grass and in the background a view of indistinct moorland. I saw as well that the grass and the graves and the moorland were the same that I had dreamed of myself seeing when I last read that page nine years ago, and when I read the page nineteen years ago.

Like most people, I dream of myself seeing places while I look at pages in books. The places are always grassy places; I do not go on looking at the pages of a book if the first pages have not made me dream of myself seeing grassy places.

I used to see the grassy places as lying somewhere on the other side of the pages I was looking at. I used to dream as though the pages I looked at were windows. I dreamed of myself seeing grassy places on the other side of every page I had looked at and of every page I would ever look at; and I dreamed of all those grassy places as being parts of one huge landscape. I was looking at pages of books only so that I could dream of myself seeing all the valleys and streams and folds of hills and heath-lands and plains in one huge grassland. A day would come, I used to suppose, when I would have looked at enough pages of books. A day would come when I could sit at this table with no pages of books in front of me and yet dream of myself surrounded by the one huge window of all the pages of books I had read, with the one huge grassland on the other side of that window.

That was what I used to suppose. But one day I was looking at a page of *Tess of the D'Urbervilles*, by Thomas Hardy. I was looking at the page and dreaming of myself seeing a young woman in a grassy place that was called the Vale of the Great Dairies but was only a small hollow in the broad grassland that I hoped to see in time from the one huge window of all the pages of books that I had read. I was dreaming of myself seeing a young woman in a grassy place, and then I saw that she was the same young woman I had dreamed of seeing when I last looked at the pages of *Wuthering Heights*, and that the grassy place was the same place I had dreamed of seeing while I read about the moorland where Catherine Earnshaw and Heathcliff had been children together.

I put *Tess of the D'Urbervilles* back in its place on my shelves, and I took down *Wuthering Heights* and looked at certain pages. At first I looked as though I was looking through window-pages, but then I saw that the young woman I saw was not even a young woman but a girl-woman and that the grassy place I saw was not a moorland but part of a paddock of grass in the district between the Moonee Ponds and the Merri. When I had seen this I was ready to acknowledge that a page of a book is not a window but a mirror. But in order to prove this finally to myself I looked for a certain page that I remembered in *Wuthering Heights*. The words on that page describe a man sleeping in a room and dreaming of the ghost of a female child who is trying to get into the room from outside by way of the window.

I stood in this room of my own and I held out in front of me the page where the word *window* is printed. If a page of a book is a window, I should have seen at that moment – in order from the nearest to my eyes to the furthest from them – the man in his room, the window of that room, and on the other side of that window the face of a female child calling herself Catherine Linton. I should have seen, while I went on looking at the page which was itself a window and which had the word *window* printed on it, the man thrusting his fist through the glass from inside outwards, then the female child gripping the man's hand with one of her own hands, then the man trying to shake his hand free from the grip of the hand of the female child, then the man dragging the wrist of the female child backwards and forwards across the edge of the broken pane until the wrist is marked by a red circle of blood.

But what I saw instead was myself in the room and a girl-woman on the other side of the window and trying to get in. I was a man whose hair had turned grey at its edges and whose belly had begun to protrude. The girl-woman was someone I had last seen when she and I were twelve years old. And I did not thrust my fist through the glass; I turned a key in one of the double panes of the window and swung the panes apart and then back against the walls of the room. Then I took hold of the wrist of the girl-woman and guided her into the room.

I had believed for most of my life that a page of a book is a window. Then I had learned that a page of a book is a mirror. I had found in more than one book a page showing me not a young woman and a grassy place in a landscape on the other side of the book but images of what was somewhere near me in this room. I had seen in the glass of more than one page the image of a girl-woman and the image of the edge of a grassland that was covered over with roads and houses thirty years ago.

I had seen images of a girl-woman and of a grassland, but I wondered where exactly were the girl-woman and the grassland that had given rise to those images.

I knew without having to look around me that not even an image of a girl-woman is visible in this room. My room contains only this table, the chair underneath me, a steel cabinet, and all the shelves of books around the walls. The shelves leave no space on the walls for pictures with images of females or of grasslands. The books have only their spines showing. But then I thought of my pages.

In all the room the only places where the images of girl-women or of grass could have appeared, I thought, were the heaps of pages on this table or the scattered pages on the floor or the margins of pages exposed in the half-opened drawers of the steel cabinet.

I have never seen, nor will I ever see, an image of a certain girl-woman or an image of certain patches of grass for as long as I sit here in front of these pages. But a man who could stand a little to one side of me and who watched my pages from the sides of his eyes and who studied not the rows of my words but the shapes of the paper showing between the words – such a man might well see an image of a girl-woman or an image of a grassland or the ghosts of such images.

That was what I supposed on the day when I wondered

where the images came from that I saw reflected in the pages of more than one book from these shelves around me. I supposed I held each book in my hands in such a way that its pages stood open at the place in the air where the face of a man would have been if the man had stood watching my own pages from the sides of his eyes.

I had learned where the images of grass and the image of a certain girl-woman had come from, but where was the girl-woman herself and where was the grass? I answered these questions by telling myself that the girl-woman and the grass were where they were – where I could see them clearly reflected from one sort of page to another. If I could not touch the hand of the girl-woman or walk through the grass, neither could I touch the hand of any other female and neither could I walk through any other grass for as long as I went on sitting in this room between the different sorts of pages.

Whatever I have written lately about images reflected from page to page is true also for echoes of sounds. Standing between these pages of mine and the pages of certain books, I have sometimes heard an echo of the sound of wind in certain grassy places or an echo of the voice of a certain girl-woman.

The sound of the wind in grass or leaves is mentioned by writers of books other than Thomas Hardy and Emily Brontë. Today I remembered a few words from the book *Indian Country*, by Peter Matthiessen, published in 1984 by Viking Press. When I found the book on my shelves I learned that the words I had remembered belong in another book. Peter Matthiessen acknowledges in a footnote that the words I had remembered belong in a work-in-progress – in a bundle of pages.

I had remembered from Peter Matthiessen's book the words of an American man who said that the wind in the leaves speaks the message: *Have no fear of the Universe.* The words belong in a bundle of pages written by a man named Peter Nabokov and called *America As Holy Land.*

I have sometimes heard in this room an echo of a sound from a word in a language other than my own.

One day I read aloud in this room a word from the spine of a book on one of these shelves around me. The word is the word for *grassland* in a language other than my own. In those days I used to dream of myself writing about grasslands; but the grasslands were in the land that I call America, and I had not dreamed of any girl-woman in the grasslands I dreamed of writing about.

The word that I read aloud sounded heavily in this room. I took the book down from the shelf and looked into the pages. Most of the words in the pages were in my own language but a few words were in the other language, and all of those words too sounded heavily when I read them aloud in this room.

I carried the book across the room to this table and I read some of its pages. They were not the first or the last pages in the book but pages deep inside the book. After

I had read the pages I got up from this table and walked to the window. I looked out across folds of hills covered with streets and houses and yards, but while I looked I was dreaming of myself looking at pages of my writing.

I came back to this table and I began to write on the first of all these pages around me, which are pages about grasslands and about a certain girl-woman.

I addressed the first of all these pages to a certain married woman of my own age. I had never seen the woman, but twenty-five years earlier she had been a girl of twelve in the district between the Moonee Ponds and the Merri. I had never thought of her as my girlfriend, but I had talked easily to her in those days.

I wrote to that woman because of all those I had known twenty-five years before, she was the only person whose whereabouts I knew. In the year before I wrote to her, or it may have been another year, I had seen by chance in a newspaper the notice of the death of the father of the girl I had once talked easily with. In the notice I had read that the man had lived until his death in a street named Daphne, which was where he and his wife and children had lived when I was twelve years old. From the same notice I had learned the name after her marriage of the girl I had once talked easily with. The name in fact was my own name. She had married a man who was unknown to me but who had the same surname as myself.

Before I wrote I learned from a telephone directory that the widow of the dead man still lived in Daphne

Street. I therefore addressed my letter to the woman with the same surname as myself, in care of the woman whose surname was still what had been the surname of the girl I had talked easily with twenty-five years before, and whose address was still what had been the address of the girl in those days.

When I looked at the envelope before I posted it, I seemed for a moment to be sending a letter to my wife – not to the wife who is in this house at the moment and somewhere on the other side of these walls covered with books, but the wife of the man who had stayed in his native district for the previous twenty-five years.

I wrote to the woman with the same name as my own that my youngest daughter had recently turned twelve years of age; that I had decided impulsively on a fine afternoon in early autumn to show my daughter the district where I had lived when I was twelve; that I had felt a trifle nostalgic as I walked along certain streets; that I found myself wondering what had happened to the children I had known in those days; that I remembered having seen in a newspaper the notice of her father's death (for which I expressed my regret); that I remembered also having learned from the same notice that her husband had the same surname as mine and that her mother still lived in Daphne Street; that I was still curious about my former schoolfriends and about two of them in particular; that I wondered whether she herself might know something of what had happened in after years to those two; that if she knew anything I would be much obliged to receive a short note from her; that the two were a boy (whom I named) who had lived in Magdalen Street and a girl (whom I named) who had lived in Bendigo Street.

As soon as I had posted my letter I persuaded myself that I would not receive a reply. I persuaded myself that the woman with the same surname as my own would see through the pretence of my letter. I supposed she would understand at once that I had never walked with my youngest daughter between the Moonee Ponds and the Merri but that I had walked there alone (and for the first time in twenty-five years) a few days before writing the letter; that I was not curious to learn what had become of the boy from Magdalen Street, although he had been one of my friends in the last months before I left my native district, but that I had learned where the boy lived as a man by looking, after I had written to her, into a telephone directory and finding his rare surname and the initials that I remembered and noting that his home was in Fawkner, only a few kilometres north of Sims Street; that I had only mentioned the boy from Magdalen Street in order to make less noticeable my asking about the other person from my schooldays; that I would not have written the letter, with its transparent lies, if I could have learned the whereabouts of the girl from Bendigo Street by simply looking into a telephone directory but that I assumed she had married long before and had changed her name and that I had noted some years earlier when I looked, as I had looked each year, into the latest edition of the telephone directory that the entry for the father of the girl at the address in Bendigo Street had been removed; that I had felt while I walked lately in the streets where I had walked twenty-five years before not a passing nostalgia but a strange mixture of feelings; that I had felt as I walked in Ray Street a mixture of sadness and shame while I dreamed of myself looking into the backyard of the ugly house and seeing the water in the pond dwindled to a shallow green sludge with the red fish lying on their sides and opening and closing their mouths and flapping their fins – or seeing my father's fowl sheds turned long since into an aviary but with the shrubs in it dead and brittle and the birds only scraps of feathers and bones by the empty water trough – or seeing the skeleton of a small dog at the end of a rusted chain; that I had felt the same mixture of sadness and shame when I walked along Sims Street and looked ahead of me as though I wondered whether I was about to see across Cumberland Road a girl-woman at a front gate with a small dog beside her.

In the days after I had posted my letter I read every page in the book with the heavy-sounding word on its cover and its spine. As soon as I had finished the last page of the book I began to write on these pages of my own. I did not expect to receive an answer to the letter that I had sent to the woman with the same surname as my own, but I wrote on my pages as though I might send the pages, all in good time, to the girl-woman I had dreamed of myself seeing by her front gate in Bendigo Street.

Twenty-five days after I had posted my letter to the woman who had once lived in Daphne Street, I received a letter in reply.

I left the reply in its sealed envelope in my steel cabinet for two weeks. I took the envelope out of my cabinet each night and looked at it and handled it. All I learned from this was that the girl who had once lived in Daphne Street in my native district had gone after her marriage to live on the far side of the Moonee Ponds. Her letter had come to me from the district between the Moonee Ponds and the Maribyrnong.

While I handled the envelope I used to dream of myself reading on the page inside (I had felt only one thin page through the envelope) the words of the writer with the same surname as myself warning me that I was doing a very strange thing – me, a man of nearly forty (as I was then), approaching a girl-woman of twelve.

Or I dreamed of myself reading that the girl from Bendigo Street had died many years before, or that she had lived for many years with her husband and children in America, or that she lived in the same district where I was living (which was only ten kilometres from the heart of my native district) and might well have passed me sometimes in a street.

Late on a night after I had been drinking beer all day, I opened the letter. I began to read it slowly, uncovering one line after another of the woman's neat handwriting.

The woman told me a little about herself and her children and her husband, who was a distant cousin of mine. In the last paragraph she told me she had gone to much trouble to find out where the boy from Magdalen Street lived. Then she told me the address that I had found one night in a few seconds by looking at the telephone directory.

After this came one short sentence before the woman thanked me for my letter and then signed her name, part of which was also part of my name. The words of the short sentence were: *I do not know where* (and here she wrote the first name only of the girl from Bendigo Street) *lives nowadays.*

I burned the envelope and the letter, and I crushed the charred paper into a powder of ashes. I swept the ashes into a jar, filled the jar with water, and stirred the water until it was a uniform dark grey. I poured the water down my kitchen sink and then ran the tap afterwards for half a minute.

Then I walked to this room and sat down at this table and began to write on one more of the pages I had still not written on.

On grasslands I almost forget my fear of drowning. Grasslands have waves and hollows, but the shape of the land under the waves is easy to dream of seeing. If the shape of a grassland changes, it changes too little to be noticed during a lifetime. When the wind makes waves in the grass, I lie under the leaning stems. I am not afraid of drowning in grass. On grasslands I have solid soil under me, and under the soil rock – the one thing I have always trusted.

I walk long distances across grasslands before I come to a creek or a river. And even I, who was always too frightened to learn to swim, can wade across a stony bed and poke a short stick into the deeper holes, and can find bottom and come out safely on the other side.

Ponds, swamps, bogs, and marshes frighten me, but I know where to look out for them. Much more alarming is to learn from seeing a subsided place or a sudden, cream-coloured cliff at my feet that for some time past, while I thought I was safe, I was walking over limestone country.

After I had written the sentence above, I remembered a thin book of poems by W. H. Auden that I had put on my shelves twenty years ago. I found the book and I turned to a long poem I had remembered as praising limestone country. I began to read the poem, but I stopped half-way through the third line of the first stanza after reading that the poet is homesick for limestone because it dissolves in water.

I did not want to read the words of a man sick, or pretending to be sick, for stone that dissolves in water. I did not want to hear from a man wanting to stand at the site of the wearing away of the thing I most trust; at the site of the melting of the most solid thing I know into the thing I am most afraid of.

I did not read any further into that poem, but I turned to another poem I had remembered: 'Plains'.

This time I read the whole of the first stanza, but I did not read past the poet's announcing that he cannot see a plain without a shudder and his pleading to God never to make him live on a plain – he would prefer to end his days on the worst of seacoasts in preference to any plain.

I put the book back on the shelf where it had stood unopened for twenty years, and I thought of all the poets who have stood on the seashores of the world watching the sea pulling idiot-faces at them or listening to the sea making idiot-noises at them. I thought the reason for my never having been able to write poetry must be that I have always kept well away from the sea. I thought of all the lines of poetry in the world as the ripples and waves of an idiot-sea, and all the sentences of prose in the world as the clumps and tussocks, leaning and waving in the wind but still showing the shape of the soil and the rock underneath, on a grassland.

I am hardly frightened of the creeks or the slow, shallow rivers of grasslands. But I prefer not to think of the underground streams of limestone country. The worst death would be to drown in a tunnel, in darkness.

I am not likely to die in limestone country. I am more likely to learn one day that the grass of the world is all one grassland. For most of my life I have looked at strips and patches of grass and weeds among the outlying streets of districts or beside railway lines or even in corners of graveyards. Or I have looked at the bare spaces between streams on maps of landlocked districts and great plains far from my own district. More likely than my being tricked by limestone country, I expect to find one day that I can walk easily across all the grasslands of the world: I can walk easily because the seas and the deep rivers have shrunk to the corners and the margins of the pages of the world.

Even the rain on grasslands seems no threat.

From a certain cloud high above the horizon a grey feather hangs down. The clouds around are whitish and drifting steadily, but one grey cloud drags a wing like a bird trying to lead the eye away.

Later a fine rain falls. The drops cling to skin, or they slide slowly down the sides of grass-stems. The feel of rain on grasslands is no more than the brushing past of a wing of water.

Whenever I want to read about the rain on grasslands, I take down from my shelves the book *Proust: A Biography*, by André Maurois, translated by Gerard Hopkins, and published by Meridian Books Inc. of New York in 1958.

In the last paragraph of that book I read the words:
Yet it is his exaltation that has brought us the perfume of the hawthorn trees that died long years ago; that has made it possible for men and women who have never seen, nor will ever see, the land of France, to breathe with ecstasy, through the curtain of the falling rain, the scent of invisible yet enduring lilacs.

Each year I take down fewer books from the shelves around me. I leave many shelves of books untouched while I look at the same few books. Of these few books the book that I look at most often is an atlas, and of all the pages in that atlas I look most often at the pages of the United States of America, which I call for convenience *America*.

Day after day I study the map of America. My right hand holds a reading-glass half-way between my eyes and the page while the index finger of my left hand travels across the page. My index finger travels slowly.

America is a huge country with many grasslands. Each state of America has so many counties, and each county has so many townships and streams, and the names of these counties and townships and streams are also the names of so many other places that I expect to spend the rest of my life tracing with my finger in the space between the town of Pysht, in Clallam County, in Washington State, and the town of Beddington, in Washington County, in the upper north-east of Maine, a summary of the lives I might have led. But if some man who is not myself stood a little to one side of me and looked from the sides of his eyes at the streams and roads between Pysht and Beddington, he might see his native district.

Four times during his life my father tried to escape into grasslands.

In the second-last year of the Second World War, when he was forty years old and living with his wife and three small sons near the east bank of Darebin Creek, he decided he was so deeply in debt that he would have to run away. Most of his debts were owed to unlicensed bookmakers who would do no more than write off my father's account when they learned he had run away.

My father travelled with his family by train across the grasslands north-west of the city of Melbourne, then through a gap in the Great Divide just west of Mount Macedon, then through hills and grasslands to the inland city of Bendigo.

My father and his wife and sons lived for four years in three different rented cottages between Bendigo Creek and Huntly Race. My father had probably intended to give up betting when he moved to this new district, but he became friendly with trainers of horses and with professional punters and bookmakers both licensed and unlicensed. At the age of forty-four, when his eldest son was nine years old, my father was once again so deeply in debt that he decided to flee.

This time my father fled south-west towards the coast. He and his wife sat in the front seat of a furniture van beside the driver while the three sons sat in the back of the van on the faded cushions from the couch and the two chairs that the family called their lounge suite.

The man drove his crowded van carefully through the hills to the inland city of Ballarat and then out into the grasslands known as the Western District. The family travelled for most of the afternoon through these grasslands. At dusk they stopped a few kilometres short of the ocean at the house my father had arranged beforehand to rent from a farmer for ten shillings a week. This was in the district between Buckley's Creek and Curdies River and only a few kilometres from where my father had been born.

The house was in a corner of one of the farmer's paddocks. No one had lived in the house for nearly a year. It had no bathroom or laundry and no sink or stove in the kitchen. When the van-driver saw the inside of the house he said without being asked that he would drive the family free of charge back to Bendigo that same night if they wanted to go back. The driver did not know that my father could not go back.

In 1951 my father was as old as I am today. He was living with his wife and their three sons in the district where the eldest son had been born. My father was living for the first time in a house that he could say was his own, but he was once again deeply in debt.

By the first week of November 1951 my father had arranged to become the manager of a farming property in a district of grasslands between the Ovens River and Reedy Creek, east of the inland city of Wangaratta. My father had not seen the property, and he had only met the owner for an hour while the man was visiting the city of Melbourne. My father was so anxious to get away that he left with his family and their furniture before the house had been sold. The sale was placed in the hands of an estate agent who was one of my father's racing acquaintances.

The family travelled in early November from the district between the Moonee Ponds and the Merri along the Hume Highway to Wangaratta. The three sons sat in the back of the van on the same cushions that they had sat on three years before. The dog Belle sat beside them, chained to a leg of the upside-down kitchen table. The boys took turns at holding on their knees a cylindrical biscuit tin full of water. In the water was a pair of goldfish, thought to be one male and one female.

In the morning while the furniture van was being loaded, the sky had been filled with clouds and the wind had been cool. But around midday the van crossed the Great Divide and the sky was suddenly clear. The Hume Highway at that time was a winding road with only two lanes for traffic. The slow-moving furniture van was followed by motor-cars around most of the winding sections of the road. The boys in the back of the van looked down through the windscreen of each motor-car and studied the faces of the people.

If the faces seemed friendly the boys waved. Sometimes the two younger boys lifted up the dog Belle and forced her to wave her paw. This made the people in the motorcars wave wildly. The two young boys wanted to devise more tricks to amuse the people. But the eldest boy, who was almost thirteen, had begun to feel somewhat ashamed that he and his family should be seen with all their belongings heaped up in a truck and the first home they had ever owned far back on the road behind them.

By mid-afternoon the sun was hot. The eldest boy recognised the dry heat of the inland that he had not felt since he had left Bendigo three years before. When the van turned aside from the empty back-road in the district between the Ovens and Reedy Creek, the faces and clothes of the boys and the fabric of the cushions were covered with golden dust as fine as face-powder. In the biscuit-tin the water had a creamy scum.

Half a kilometre back from the back-road, a house

stood among fruit trees and green lawns. The house looked to have at least six large rooms under its broad roof of dark-green iron. The doors and windows of the house were deep in shadow beneath a veranda that ran along the front and one side of the house. Much of this veranda was hidden behind the green leaves of creepers.

The eldest boy got to his feet in the back of the van. When he stood up, dust fell out of the folds of his clothes. He looked at the sprawling house of brown-red weatherboards under a dark-green roof and a cloudless sky of deep blue. He saw that this could well have been one of the houses he had dreamed of himself living in after he had married and gone to live in grasslands.

A woman came out from among the green creepers at the side of the house. She had grey hair, and she seemed old to the boys in the back of the van, but she would have been no older than I am today. She handed an orange to each of the boys and said a few friendly words. The boys thanked her from out of their masks of golden dust.

The woman went to the front of the van and introduced herself to my father, who had stepped down from the cabin. She was the wife of the owner of the property, and she lived in the house with the creepers on the veranda. If my father would direct the van-driver around the next corner in the driveway and then on towards the farm buildings, he would find the farm-manager's house empty and waiting with the key in the door.

The woman went back in among the creepers. My

father climbed back into the van and the driver drove on.

The house that was waiting for us was a weatherboard cottage of four small rooms. The rooms were clean, and the kitchen had a sink and a stove, but what astonished my father and mother and the van-driver and even the three boys was that the cottage was adjoined on two sides by sheep yards.

At the front of the cottage and at one of its sides a small lawn grew – a patch of green grass two or three paces wide. The lawn was fenced around with a strong wire and timber fence that was clearly meant to keep out wandering cattle. But on the other two sides of the cottage no fence stood and no grass grew; the brown weatherboard walls of the cottage itself served as part of the outer fence of a maze of sheep yards connected with the silver-grey shearing shed about forty paces away.

When the parents looked inside the cottage they learned that one of the walls adjoining the sheep yards was the wall of the room that would be their lounge room. The single window of this room looked out at the sheep yards and the shearing shed. My mother stepped across the bare boards of the empty room and pushed open the single pane of the window. She put her head through the window and looked across the yards. The surface of the yards was finely trampled dust and dried sheep-dung. The sill of the window was low enough for a sheep to have rested its front feet there and to have looked inside in the same way that my mother had looked out.

The driver of the van did not offer to drive the family back to the city of Melbourne; and even if he had offered, my father would not have gone back. My mother, however, announced to my father that she would not live in that house. She would consent to store the furniture in the house and to eat and sleep there until my father had arranged to get the family back to some district near Melbourne; but she would unpack only what was needed for cooking and eating meals, because she was not going to live in the cottage by the sheep yards.

The driver and my father and the three boys unloaded the van. My mother unpacked the tea chests that contained crockery and cutlery and pillows and bed-coverings. But for two weeks while the family lived in the cottage nothing else was unpacked – except that the three boys took out the glass fish tank that their mother had bought for them in their last days in the district between the Moonee Ponds and the Merri. They rested the glass tank on a nailed-down tea chest in the lounge-room under the window that looked out onto the dirt and the dried dung, and they carried jugs of water from the rainwater tank outside the house and filled the fish tank and poured in the water from the biscuit tin and the two red fish that had survived in it.

Fifteen days after the family had arrived in the district between the Ovens and Reedy Creek, they loaded their belongings into another van. Most of the tea chests had not been opened since the day when a van had brought the family and their belongings inland from the district between the Moonee Ponds and the Merri. The fish tank had been emptied again and the fish poured into the biscuit tin.

The house with the fish pond on the back lawn had been sold. The father had not even considered going back. The family was going to live in a district where none of them had been before – the district of swamps and tea-tree scrub between Scotchman's Creek and Elster Creek. A racing acquaintance of the father was a builder of houses in that district. He would build a cheap house for the family on a cheap block of land among the tea-tree and the stands of watsonia lilies and the prickly manuka scrub. But the building of the house might take six months. In the meanwhile the family would live separately with relatives in districts on three sides of the city of Melbourne. The eldest son would be sent to the district between the Moonee Ponds and the Merri.

In 1960, when he was nine years older than I am now, my father made his last attempt to escape into grasslands.

He was still living in the district between Scotchman's Creek and Elster Creek, but only his wife and his youngest son were still living with him. He was not in debt. He had fallen deeply into debt four years before, but at that time he had chosen not to run away. Instead he had gone to work by night as well as by day to pay back his debts to bookmakers.

For four years my father had worked at two jobs. On

many nights during those four years he slept for only two or three hours. At the end of the four years he had paid his debts but he was tired. He sold his house in the district between Scotchman's Creek and Elster Creek, and he and his wife and his youngest son went to live between Sutherland's Creek and Hovell's Creek, on the edge of the plains known as the Western District. He told his friends that he wanted not to work so hard in future.

In the winter of that year my father bought a motor-car. He drove in his motor-car all around the district between Hopkins River and Buckley's Creek where he had been born and had spent part of his childhood. Then he returned to his home on the edge of the plains and fell ill and died quietly, after which his body was buried on the west bank of the Hopkins River, near where that river flows into the sea.

M

aps of my native district nowadays show a small dead-end street named Ryland leading west from the Hume Highway near the North Coburg tram terminus. Thirty-five years ago the land now covered by the street and its houses was one of the last few grasslands in my native district.

I arrived on that grassland in November 1951, and I lived there for two months in a large weatherboard house with a veranda at the front and along one side. I was brought to the weatherboard house in a motor-car. My parents had told me to travel there by tram from the furniture-storage depot where the van-driver had set us down on the afternoon when we returned from the district between the Ovens and Reedy Creek. But the people from the weatherboard house had called for me in their motor-car after they had learned I would be carrying not only my suitcase but a biscuit-tin with two goldfish.

The people in the weatherboard house were related to my father by marriage, but until I went to live with them I had hardly known them. My father had told me they were kindly people but religious maniacs. He was a loyal Catholic himself, but he disliked any public show or ceremony.

The old weatherboard house had been built as a farm-house fifty years before. Of the farm, one paddock of grass still remained, as well as a row of tumbledown sheds and one other building of a kind I had never seen before.

About thirty paces from the back door of the house, and about half-way from the house to where the dairy had once stood, I found what my relatives called the coolroom. From the rear or from either side, the coolroom seemed an artificial hill rising abruptly from the backyard: a hill of white flowers with tufts of grass showing between them. From the front, I saw an open doorway flanked on each side by a slope of the flowery hill and looking like the entrance to a symmetrical tunnel in the papier mâché landscape around a model railway.

The doorway had once been filled by a heavy door, but when I saw it the doorway was only an opening with darkness behind it. When I walked through the doorway I was in a curving tunnel paved and walled and roofed with blocks of blue-black basalt. The tunnel was about two metres from floor to ceiling and its plan was a simple curve:

about one eighth of the circumference of a circle. The tunnel was always empty; the people of the weatherboard house had no use for it. When I had walked to the end of it and turned around, I found I was just out of sight of the entrance. I stood in mild twilight, with the bright summer daylight just around the bend in front of me.

Blue-black basalt is the rock that underlies the district between the Moonee Ponds and the Merri. I would never have dared to go down a mine or a well to see into the heart of my native district, but the coolroom behind the former farmhouse seemed a safe and inviting place. I stood for two or three minutes every day with my back against the end of the short tunnel and my hands against the basalt blocks. While I felt the stone against my palms and against the back of my head and the calves of my legs, I thought of someone looking out just then from a window of one of the trains that passed all day between Batman and Merlynston stations.

The trains passed close beside the weatherboard house. The view from the railway line was across the paddock of grass and into the backyard of the house, but the coolroom faced away from the railway line. I thought every day of a passenger looking across the paddock and seeing the small abrupt hill rising from the grass. I thought of a passenger who happened to be interested in grasslands and who thought that the flowers growing in clumps on the small abrupt hill might have been the last few of a rare kind of flower that had once flourished in the district. That passenger would never have thought, I thought, of myself hiding all the while under the flowers and the tufts of grass and inside my dry well.

One of the women from the weatherboard house helped me to find in the long grass of the backyard an old laundry trough. I cleaned the soil out of the trough and dragged it into the shade of a tree and filled it with water and kept the two goldfish in it for as long as I stayed in the weatherboard house.

The same woman told me that the flowers growing on the sides of the coolroom were called Chinese mignonette. She told me other names of flowers that I had not known before. The name that most interested me was love-in-a-mist. I would have liked to meet the person who had looked sideways at a few green feathery strands and had seen a mist and who had looked sideways at a blue-petalled flower and had seen love.

The namer of love-in-a-mist would have understood, I thought, why I looked every day from the sides of my eyes at a small plant with bunched leaves of glossy dark-green and red. A row of these plants formed a border by a path.

The woman who had earlier named the flowers for me saw me looking one day at the row of plants by the path. The woman told me that the plants were a sort of begonia. She must have thought I was interested in the pink flowers of the begonia rather than the green and red leaves, because she took me to the bookshelves in the room she called the parlour and opened the glass doors and reached down a book by W. H. Hudson. The woman then showed me two passages from one of the essays in the book.

I have found today in my own copy of the same book what I believe were the passages I was shown in the weatherboard house.

...the expression peculiar to red flowers varies infinitely in degree, and is always greatest in those shades of the colour which come nearest to the most beautiful flesh-tints...

The blue flower is associated, consciously or not, with the human blue eye; and as the floral blue is in all or nearly all instances pure and beautiful, it is like the most beautiful eye...

The woman told me that most people keep throughout their lives the memory of the soft skin and the loving eyes of their mothers. I listened politely but I did not believe the woman. I had been looking at the leaves of the begonia because I connected the green and the red with water and fish.

On another day the woman showed me another book. I have since learned that the book was *The Language of Flowers*, illustrated by Kate Greenaway and published (undated) by Frederick Warne and Company, London and New York. The woman told me I could find in that book what she called the meaning of my favourite flowers. I was not interested in the book then, but a month ago when

I saw a copy of the book I looked for two plants that I have named on some of these pages. Beside *lilac* I read: *the first emotions of love*. Beside *tamarisk* I read: *crime*.

After a few days in the weatherboard house I understood why my father had called our relatives religious maniacs.

The people of the weatherboard house had been, five years before, among the founders of a utopian settlement in the mountains between King River and Broken River. When I was at the weatherboard house the settlement in the mountains was going through hard times and some of the founders had left, but almost every week a new recruit – a young man or a young woman – would call at the house on the way to join the settlement.

I thought these people were far from being religious maniacs. If it had been possible I would have gone off myself to the community in the mountains. I thought of it as a landscape from mediaeval Europe transplanted to the headwaters of the King River. The settlers went to mass each morning in their chapel; by day they tended their herds or tilled their crops; at night they practised arts and crafts or discussed theology. Living simple and virtuous lives in the mountains, the settlers would not have been afraid if they had seen the signs in the sky of the end of the world.

The people in the weatherboard house talked often about Europe. They bought strangely shaped loaves of bread and strangely coloured sausages in the suburb of

Carlton. They drank wine with their evening meal. They often said that the lives of most Catholics around them lacked ceremony and richness.

I arrived at the weatherboard house on a Saturday. That same evening I was invited to help weave a wreath from the grey branches and the green leaves of a fig-tree. When the wreath had been woven, red candles were stood upright among the branches and the leaves. The whole was then hung by thin wires from the chandelier in the centre of the parlour. I was told that this was an Advent wreath and that every Catholic household in Europe hung such a thing during the season of Advent.

Every night the people of the weatherboard house gathered in the parlour for prayers. On the night when the Advent wreath had been hung, they added to their prayers a hymn with Latin words and a sad melody. Today, thirty-five years later, I remember only the first words of that mournful song for Advent:

Rorate coeli desuper
Et nubes pluant justum.

I was told that the words might have been translated as:

Drop down dew, ye heavens,
and let the clouds sprinkle
rain on the just one.

I was told also that the words of the hymn ought to be understood as the yearning of the people of the Old Testament for the Saviour who would be born at Christmas. Yet the song made me think not of the Jews wandering among rocks and sand but of a woebegone tribe wandering like gipsies across an immense grassland under low grey clouds.

I had not been to church since I had left the house with the fish pond on the lawn. In the district between the Ovens and Reedy Creek we had had no motor-car and my father had said we were surely to be excused from having to attend mass, which was fifteen kilometres away in Wangaratta. When I arrived at the weatherboard house I could not have said what week had been reached in the church year. Seeing the wreath being made, I thought Advent must have arrived already; but I was not going to appear ignorant by asking the expert Catholics around me.

Next morning, which was a Sunday morning, I learned that the people of the house had woven their wreath and sung their hymn a few days early for Advent. In the parish church of Saint Mark, Fawkner, the priest strode out to the altar in bright green. The Sunday was the last of the season after Pentecost, and when the gospel was read I heard from the fifteenth through to the thirty-fifth verse of the twenty-fourth chapter of the Gospel of Saint Matthew.

*When you shall see the abomination
of desolation, which was spoken of by Daniel the Prophet, standing in
the holy place (he that readeth, let him understand)...*

These words, like most of the words of my religion,
had many meanings. Whenever I heard these words as
a child, I was standing myself in the holy place: in a
large weatherboard church in McCrae Street, Bendigo;
or in a tiny church with poles propping its walls on the
continuation inland of the Great Ocean Road at Nirranda;
or in the fibro-cement and weatherboard church-school
in Landells Road, Pascoe Vale. I was standing in the holy
place and hearing the words, but I had my missal open in
my hands – I was also reading. I was he who reads: he who
was commanded to understand.

Around me in the church, hundreds of other people – children and adults – were reading the same words that I was reading. Yet I had no doubt that I was the one commanded to understand; I was of all those readers the true reader.

I was the true reader because I had always known that everything I read was true. If it was not true in the district between the Moonee Ponds and the Merri, or wherever I happened to be standing or sitting when I read, still it was true in some district elsewhere.

When I had read those words in weatherboard churches or in the fibro-cement and weatherboard church-school, I had understood that all the districts of the world would one day be destroyed. At some time before the end, the people of all the districts of the world would flee from their homes; they would flee with their few sticks of furniture and their rags of clothes, but they would not escape. The people of every district would suffer, and the females would suffer worst. Then, while the people were still fleeing, they would see Jesus himself: the person who had first spoken the words that had later been written by Matthew. The people trying to escape would see, towards the end, the true speaker of the words they had once read, coming in the clouds of heaven with much power and majesty.

Whenever I had read the gospel for the last Sunday after Pentecost I had seen a sky darkening, men and their wives and children fleeing, and then the grey clouds of heaven drifting towards the people. But without lifting my eyes from the page, I knew that the sky was mostly blue over the district where I was standing; I knew that men were pushing lawnmowers across their backyards and women were opening the doors of ovens and then pouring cups of water into baking-dishes where legs of lamb or rolls of beef were roasting. I knew that these men and women saw no clouds drifting towards them.

Yet what I read was true. Somewhere the clouds were drifting, and one day he who reads would look up and see the sky of the gospel drifting towards him and would know then that he had always understood. He would know then that the tribes of the earth were about to mourn and that the stars were about to fall from heaven. He would know that angels were about to gather the elect from the four winds. He would know also that when the end had almost arrived he would think for the last time about the fig-tree. Wherever I stood in my native district in the year before I turned thirteen, I thought of my girlfriend as watching me from somewhere just behind my left shoulder. My chief pleasure for much of that year was to feel myself watched by the girl-woman I called my girlfriend. Yet along with my pleasure I felt a mild sadness. I called the girl at my shoulder by the same name as the girl from Bendigo Street but I knew she was not the same girl.

The two girls looked alike, and their voices sounded alike, but they were not the same girl. Even after the girl from Bendigo Street had sat with me in our classroom on a certain rainy afternoon and we had exchanged messages without looking at one another – even after that day the two girls were not the same. I still said more to the girl at my shoulder than I had said to the girl from Bendigo Street, and I believed that the girl at my shoulder could have said more to me than the girl from Bendigo Street could have said.

On Sunday afternoons when I stood among the puddles in Sims Street and I looked north across the grass and saw at the same time from the sides of my eyes the reddish blur of the brick veneer houses just across Cumberland Road to my left, I was pleased to be about to walk the last few paces to Bendigo Street. I was pleased to be about to stand by a front gate and to see two black boots by a front door. But I seemed to be about to disturb somewhat the proper arrangement of the world around me.

Between me and the grass and the sky and the houses of my native district was another layer of places, and in that other layer was the girl who watched from my shoulder. On most Sunday afternoons a moment arrived when I stood so that the two girls were at the same angle behind me, the girl at my shoulder occupying a place in her layer of places such that she was directly between me and the place further away where the girl from Bendigo Street was waiting to hear her dog bark as I walked past. Perhaps at that moment I should have supposed that the layers of the world were in their true positions, and that the layer of places nearer to me – and the girl who watched me from out of that layer – was only a layer of signs that should have guided me to the further layer and the girl waiting in that layer to hear her dog bark. But I was more likely to think at such moments that the many layers of the world could have been easily dislodged. Even if I did not think of the girl and her parents fleeing from Bendigo Street to the mountains or of the stars falling from heaven or of the elect being gathered from the four winds, I was still likely to think of the layers around me as being easily dislodged. I was likely to make myself sure of the layer of the world that was nearest me, and of the girl who watched me from that layer of the world, in case I found one day that the other layer of the world was not where I had last seen it.

When we were told by our teacher in the winter of 1951 that several hundred Balts had arrived in our district and that some of the Balt children would be coming to our school, I was the only boy or girl who knew where the Baltic Sea was and what were the names of the three Baltic countries.

In the atlas among my schoolbooks, Ireland was still the Irish Free State, Danzig was still a Free City, and three separate countries, neatly shaped and distinctively coloured, rested one on top of the other by the pale-blue Baltic Sea. Sometimes I thought I could have given up my ambition to be a trainer or a breeder of racehorses in a mansion surrounded by grasslands if I could have become a professor of geography in a university. I thought of a university as a secular monastery fenced around by high brick walls and iron spikes. Far away inside the walls and the spikes, at the heart of a maze of lawns and ferneries and flower-beds and ornamental lakes, the professors and their students sat in book-lined rooms. The student of geography was required, by the end of the course, to have memorised the world in considerable detail. At the final examination blank paper and coloured pencils were provided for the student to reproduce remote islands and landlocked countries.

In my years at primary school I had never earned less than perfect marks for what my teachers called geography. Every week in the period known as free reading I read my atlas. I learned so easily what I read, and yet I saw so many thousands of items waiting to be learned, that I assumed I could have made my life's work the study of this vast body of knowledge. My studies would make me in time a man who was the admiration of students and colleagues: a man who could talk for hours in the language of the atlas until the air around me was thick with invisible layers of maps.

Each day in my book-lined room at the university, my students ply me with questions. Today they ask me about Idaho. I lean back in my chair and I wrinkle my forehead. The hearts of the young female students especially go

out to me when I lower my eyelids and recite, as easily as
though I read from a compendious volume, the names of
a myriad of streams and a veritable patchwork of districts
in the Bitterroot Range.

When I had no map in front of me I saw the Baltic
countries as grey – the grey of the smoke drifting over
all the bombed cities of Europe, or of the rats that the
Europeans had had to eat as food during the war.

Three Balt children arrived at my school: two girls
and a boy. The girls were put in my class although they
seemed older than my classmates and myself. Both girls
had well-rounded breasts. The Balts were not the only
girls in my school with breasts, but the two girls seemed
more graceful and womanly than any schoolgirls I had
known.

The boys and girls of my school hung back from the
children of the Baltic countries, but I went up to the
girls to talk to them. Their faces interested me. I had not
expected such clear skin and such serene smiles on girls
from the grey, ruined cities of Europe, and I could never
have believed that those two girls had eaten rats.

I showed the girls a certain page in my atlas. Then
I turned aside and recited without looking at the page the
names of the three Baltic countries and their capital cities.
Each girl clasped her hands in front of her breasts and
smiled and thanked me. When I saw that I had touched
them I felt an urge to protect them – I a twelve-years-old

boy in short pants and they two buxom thirteen- or fourteen-years-old young women with a wise sadness behind their smiles. I wanted to warn the Balt girls not to expect to find anyone else at the school who was interested in Europe. I wanted to protect the Balts from hearing the older boys talking filth, as they sometimes did. I wanted to keep the Balts from seeing in certain streets of my district the few shabby houses that I called slums. I wanted to teach the Balts my own language so that no one would laugh at their odd speech. I wanted to talk with them about all they had seen during the war – not to distress them but to remind them that they were safe now between the Moonee Ponds and the Merri, with only grey clouds passing sometimes overhead.

I was drawn to the young Baltic women but I would have been angry and embarrassed if anyone had said they were my girlfriends. From the day when I had met the Balts, the sight of their breasts had forbidden me to think of the young women as anything other than friends of mine. The two Balts were my friends, although they sometimes smiled at one another while I was with them as though they were two aunts and I was their favourite nephew.

I asked the two young women to teach me their language in exchange for my teaching them the language of my district. For my first lesson they brought to school and invited me to borrow a small book about their homeland. The book had parallel texts in my language and theirs. The young women wanted me to take the book home and to learn the words of their national anthem in their language and in mine.

I was reluctant to take the book at first. It was only thin and bound with paper, but the pictures in it were tinted in rich, autumnal colours. I turned the pages and saw green-black forests, blue lakes with red-gold reedbeds; many-roomed country houses and castles; cobbled streets and horse-drawn carts. I thought the book might have been an heirloom, but today I suppose it was something prepared and printed after the war and distributed hastily by people who feared that a whole country was on the way to disappearing.

I wrapped the book carefully before I took it home. All afternoon and evening I studied the two sets of words for the anthem. I wanted to amaze the young women next morning by reciting their own words faultlessly. After that they would teach me more of their strange language. I would duplicate everything I knew; I would discover a second name for everything in my native district for grass and sky and clouds and even the puddles underfoot.

I decided I would teach the Baltic language to my girlfriend. She would have scoffed if I had suggested we learn it openly in the schoolground, but every Sunday afternoon I would teach her a little. I had forgotten the hundreds of Balts in my district who spoke the language that I was learning. I was thinking of my new language as a secret code. I foresaw my young aunts teaching me the words for *love* and *deeply* and *dream*.

I spoke that night in the Baltic language to my father. I recited to him the first line of the national anthem of the homeland of the two young women. The equivalent words in my own language are:

Land of ours! Land of the noble heroes!

I should have known what my father would say. When I had told him the meaning of the words I had learned and the name of the country they referred to, my father said he was pleased to say that he had never before heard the name of that country, much less the name of any noble hero the country had produced.

My father spoke fiercely but not unkindly. Such countries had no heroes. Such countries had only slaves and masters. If he and I had been born in any such country, my father said, we would have had to bow and scrape and doff our caps left, right, and centre as soon as we had stepped out of our front door in the morning. The duke or the earl or the lord of the manor could have sent his lackeys into our house to take the bread off our table or the money out of our pockets or even our sisters or daughters out of their beds.

It was not my father's words that dissuaded me from learning the Baltic language. When I tried to recite their national anthem to the young women next morning I was trying to pronounce words that I had read but had never heard spoken. The young women were embarrassed for my sake when I rattled off my strange sounds. We understood that we would have to begin again by saying very simple

things to one another; but after a few days the young
women had made friends with some of the older girls and
I was playing football with the boys.

The young Balt boy at my school grinned at me but knew
hardly any words of my language. He was the only male
Balt I had seen, but I understood that hordes of young
Balt men were living in a cluster of grey buildings that
looked like a disused factory in Cumberland Road. Almost
as soon as I had heard about the Balt men, I heard that
some of the men had been walking up boldly to young
women in the streets of my district and even to some of
the older schoolgirls and asking the young women or the
girls to go with them down the steep hill where Bell Street
ended at the Moonee Ponds Creek.

I knew a boy who lived in Magdalen Street, almost at the
edge of the steep hill. Every day the boy called on the Balts
in their grey buildings, so he told me. He showed me empty
cigarette tins and tobacco tins that he said the Balts had
given him. I had collected myself many kinds of cigarette
tins and tobacco tins, but I had never seen the strange
foreign tins that the Balts had used. I washed my hands
after touching the tins, in case they were contaminated by
some European disease.

One dark afternoon in winter I walked beside the
boy from Magdalen Street to stare at the Balts' buildings.
The boy told me that the Balts he knew would not be
home from work yet, and for that reason we could only

walk among the grey buildings without going inside. The buildings were by then almost black against the weak, yellowish sunset. I wondered whether the yard had always been muddy and the buildings shabby or whether the Balts had dirtied the place since they had arrived there from Europe.

The boy beside me picked up a tobacco tin from a heap of rubbish near a hut. On all our walk I saw no Balt men, although I heard voices from inside one of the huts.

We walked away from the huts and south along Cumberland Road to Bell Street. We turned right at Bell Street and walked to the ragged wire fence and the NO ROAD sign. We climbed through the fence and walked across the grass to the place where the ground fell away.

My district was quiet in those days. We heard only an occasional hum from a motor-car far away. The Moonee Ponds Creek was below us, in its deep valley. The district on the other side was mostly marked by streets of houses, as my own district was marked, but the streets were already deep in shadow. The aerodrome, which I had never seen, was just out of sight behind a plateau. Where the valley opened out towards the south-east was the raised wooden circuit of a bicycle racing track, and near it was the ellipse of white grit where the greyhounds raced at Napier Park.

The other side of the valley seemed a strange and lonely place to me, even though I had been born only a half-hour's walk from the Moonee Ponds. I supposed the valley would have seemed a desolate place to a Balt. I thought of one of the Balt men walking to the edge of the valley from his black buildings and then looking west towards his land of the noble heroes. The Balt would crumple; he would burst into tears, I thought, to see districts so strange and to think of all the young women in those districts who had not even seen the Baltic countries in an atlas.

Just in front of me was the first clump of gorse bushes. This was what we had come to see, my friend told me. Every Saturday and Sunday afternoon since the Balts had first arrived in our district, the gorse on the hillside had been crowded, according to the boy from Magdalen Street, with what he called shaggers. The Balt men were crazy about shagging. They had been locked in prison camps since the end of the war, and now they were taking the young women of our district into the gorse bushes above the Moonee Ponds and shagging them to their hearts' content.

In the winter of 1951 I knew that men and women fitted their bodies together much as dogs or cattle did. I knew which part of my body was meant to fit into a female body and I knew what shape that part of me had to take before it could fit. But although I had peered closely sometimes between the legs of a female child, I had never touched what I saw there. I had never thought of that female part as having any shape other than the shape I had seen. I thought of that part as a fissure, a narrow opening no wider than the slot of a money box. The flesh around the opening I thought of as hairless, white, and as firm as the back of a hand. During the fitting together of male and female, the male part would have been pushed, I thought, with much effort against the female part until at last the mere tip of the male part was wedged for a crucial moment between the two unyielding doors of the female.

All this was a natural parallel of the act of kissing, I thought. I had seen characters kissing in a few films but I had not observed them closely. I thought at the age of twelve and for nearly ten years afterwards that the act of kissing was the pressing together of sealed lips.

In the district between the Moonee Ponds and the Merri in the year 1951, I foresaw myself kissing the girl from Bendigo Street when we were perhaps fifteen years old, marrying her when we were twenty-one, and afterwards pressing our bodies together every month or so. In bed at night in the year when I foresaw these things, I sometimes pressed my thumb and the base of my index finger together to make what I supposed was a replica of the female part; I then pushed with my swollen boy's part against the narrow aperture. I pushed until I was tired and angry but the gap had not widened.

When the Balts shagged the females of our district, the men from Europe wore sheaths of golden rubber over themselves.

My friend, the boy from Magdalen Street, decided one day to teach me all I needed to know about men and women. Not much of what he told me was new to me, but I was astonished to hear about the yellow rubber. I was also confused, and the boy who instructed me was sometimes vague himself. I believed the Balt men wore rubber over themselves as much from bravado as from fear of impregnating the young women of our district. I also believed that the rubber would have inflicted at least a mild pain on the young women. And I believed that no one else in our district before the coming of the Balts had worn rubber: the Balts, I thought, had brought their sheaths of gold rubber, like their strangely coloured tobacco tins and their invisible European germs, from their grey homeland.

I wanted to learn the worst I could learn about the Balts, with their heads shaped like soccer balls and their vicious blue eyes. I wanted to see them wearing their gold armour.

On Saturday afternoons in the year when I was twelve, I was allowed to go with boys I knew to the Tasma cinema in Bell Street. The audience was mostly children, but some of the older boys had their girlfriends sitting in their laps. After I had heard how the Balt men spent their Saturday afternoons, I did not want to sit among the screaming kids in the Tasma. I told the boy from Magdalen Street I would spend the next Saturday afternoon with him, looking out for shaggers in the gorse above the Moonee Ponds.

On an afternoon when my mother thought I was watching *Curtain Call at Cactus Creek*, I went to the house of the boy in Magdalen Street. He pointed out that the weather was not really shaggers' weather. Too many grey clouds were drifting in from the west and threatening rain. But I would not be talked out of going.

At the top of the hill the boy told me he sometimes ran down through the gorse screaming and howling. When he did this, the boy said, a Balt would jump up from behind every bush with his trousers clutched around him. All the Balts would jump off the girls they were shagging; they would stagger to their feet to see what the terrible noise was. Today though, the boy told me, we would walk quietly and perhaps creep up on some of the shaggers.

The boy and I found signs that people had been on the hillside recently – a broken length of comb and a crushed ball of a handkerchief in a snug place among the waist-high bushes – but we saw no shaggers. Yet when we reached the creek at the bottom of the valley, the boy pointed behind me and I saw, high on the hill, the head and shoulders of a man looking around him.

The man was too far away for me to be sure that he was a Balt, but he went on looking around as though he belonged where he stood. I thought I recognised the moment when he noticed the two boys looking up at him from beside the creek, and I was surprised that he did not drop down at that moment but went on staring as though we two boys were the intruders.

I tried to imagine the lower parts of the man, and the yellow part of him pointing upwards in the shade of the gorse bushes. I waited to see the head and shoulders of a young woman appearing beside the man – perhaps some young woman that I had passed every day in the streets of my district. But the women were more cautious than the Balts, the boy had told me; the women always stayed hidden.

After the boy and I had turned away, I wondered whether the man had been a Balt after all. I thought he might have been a man whose girlfriend had been stolen by the Balts and who had come to torment himself by looking around the hillside where some Baltic brute had worked on the young woman with his barbarous yellow rubber.

I walked with the boy from Magdalen Street north along the Moonee Ponds, mostly following the east bank but sometimes crossing the stream at a shallow ford of stones and gravel. The boy showed me pools where he and his friends had swum naked, caves in cliffs where they had smoked cigarettes, beaches where they had sunned themselves in summer or grilled sausages over camp fires in winter.

By a deep pool a man stood with a net on a long pole. He dragged the net through the water close to the bank and then hoisted it out of the water and up into the air. The man held the net under his chin and peered into it. When we asked him, the man said he was looking for skipjacks, which he said were half-grown dragonflies. He asked us did we ever go fishing. When we said we did not, he said nothing more to us and dipped his net again.

The course of the creek swerved and twisted. I became

pleasantly confused. I could see grey fences of backyards on a green clifftop, but I could not have said which part of my native district I was looking at. Already I was thinking of myself looking afterwards at a map and trying to follow my route beside the creek with a finger gliding across a page. That day was one of many days in my life when I have wanted to be at the same time myself lost in my surroundings and myself looking afterwards at maps that explain not only where I was but why I supposed at the time that I was elsewhere.

That was also one of many days when I reminded myself that the pattern of streets and footpaths laid over my district was only one of many patterns that might have been laid over it. Creeks and rivers offered hints of other patterns I had never seen. I might well have thought I could return to the valley of the Moonee Ponds whenever I wanted to see such hints of other patterns. I could never have supposed in 1951 that the shape of the Moonee Ponds itself would be changed in my lifetime, in order to allow a road known as a freeway to pass along the valley where boys from my school had swum naked and a man had netted skipjacks among the water plants.

The boy and I rested on a beach of coarse sand by a bend in the creek. The boy was a few months older than myself. Like myself he was acknowledged to have a girlfriend. But whereas my girlfriend was thin and angular, his girl had the beginnings of curves on her body. Without meeting the eye of the boy from Magdalen Street, and as lightly as I could ask, I asked him had he ever brought his girlfriend down to the creek.

The boy might have told me almost any sort of story and I would have believed it or pretended to believe it. Instead, he knelt and began smoothing the sand around him with wide sweeps of his forearm and then with short, fanning movements of the hand such as I had used in my backyard between Bendigo Creek and Huntly Race in order to clear the ground before I built a racecourse and stud properties on my first grasslands.

The boy drew with a twig on the sand an outline of the torso of a human female. He drew the shoulders and the hips hastily but he worked with care on the two breasts, and he sifted handfuls of pebbles at the edge of the creek before he found two stones suitable for resting on the sandy mounds as nipples.

I smoothed my own patch of sand and drew a figure like the figure drawn by the boy from Magdalen Street. While I was scraping up two small hills for the breasts I was uneasy. I had assumed that the figure drawn in the sand by the boy beside me was meant to represent his girlfriend, but I did not want the boy to assume that I was drawing in the sand the girl from Bendigo Street. I had not thought who the female might be, or even whether she was girl or woman. And even if I had been forced to say that the female in the sand was the girl I was in love with, I would have preferred not to say whether the male kneeling above the female was myself or the man of Europe who would get her as soon as she was old enough.

The boy had sketched the outlines of two parted thighs. Now he knelt carefully between the thighs and began to dig a small hole with his fingers. He made the hole as deep as his fingers were long, and he tried to keep the hole neatly cylindrical.

Until the boy had begun to dig the hole, I had thought he knew the female body well. Now I thought the boy knew hardly more than I knew. I thought the boy was digging in the sand the steep-sided hole he would have liked to find between female thighs rather than the much narrower opening that was actually there.

He lay down over his female. He reached one hand underneath himself and, so far as I could see, pretended to take out what I had heard him on other days call his jock. Then he pushed with his hips as I supposed he had seen male dogs pushing against bitches.

Watching him, I had a moment of recklessness. I thought of myself digging an even more preposterous hole than the boy had dug and of flinging myself against it to outdo him. But the moment passed, and when the boy from Magdalen Street got to his feet I was already wiping away the outlines I had drawn.

There was no hole for me to fill – I had not even begun to dig into the sand. After I had smoothed away the thighs and the torso I had only to toss the two pebble-nipples into the Moonee Ponds and then to make the low hills of breasts level again with the plains around them.

And from the fig-tree learn a parable: when the branch thereof is now tender, and the leaves come forth, you know the summer is nigh. So likewise you, when you shall see all these things, know that it is nigh, even at the doors.

Even the gospel was more than one gospel. The reading for the last Sunday after Pentecost began with the abomination of desolation and with a warning to the reader. For three quarters of its length, the gospel for that last Sunday of the year continued to warn. Near the end came the clouds and the four winds, and then the last pause before the ultimate turmoil. And in that last pause, startlingly under the terrible sky, the fig-tree appeared, with its leaves coming forth.

More clearly than anything I read or heard in my childhood, that last pause near the end of the last gospel of the year told me that every thing would always be more than one thing. The last pause told me that every thing would always contain another thing, which would contain still another thing or which would seem, absurdly at first sight, to contain the thing that had seemed to contain it.

Five years after I had heard the last gospel of the ecclesiastical year in the parish church of Saint Mark, Fawkner, I listened for the first time in my life to a piece of what I called classical music. Near the end of that music I heard a pause. The solemn themes of the music paused for a moment. Just before the clouds had drifted over all the sky and just before the four winds whistled and the last struggle began, I heard the pause of the summer that seemed nigh.

I have heard that pause many times since in pieces of music. I have heard the pause while I read the next-to-last page in many a book. The larger, the solemn themes are about to go into battle for the last time. By now, of course, the solemn themes are not themes but men and women, and when they pause for the last time they look over their shoulders.

They look back towards some district where they lived as children or where they once fell in love. Perhaps they see the green lawn or even the branch with green leaves that they saw in their native district. For a moment a simple theme is the only theme heard; the greenness appears in place of the greyness.

For an absurd moment within that moment, the listener or the reader dares to suppose that this after all is the last theme; this and not the other is the end; the green has outlasted the grey; the grey has been covered over at last by the green.

But this is only a moment within a moment. The clouds resume their drifting; the four winds whistle. The solemn themes turn to meet the storm.

T*hen let them that are in Judaea flee to the mountains...*

In the spring of 1951 I first saw the leaves coming forth on the fig-tree in my backyard two months before I heard the fig-tree mentioned in the gospel. When I first saw the leaves I was living in the house with the fish pond behind it. I could not have imagined when I first saw the leaves that before I heard the gospel I would have travelled two hundred kilometres across the Great Divide to the district between the Ovens and Reedy Creek and then back again to the old weatherboard house on the edge of a grassland near the backyard where my father had held me for my first photograph.

I heard the last gospel of the church year only a

half-hour's walk from where I had seen the leaves on the fig-tree but I knew while I heard the gospel that I would never see that particular fig-tree again – or the house with the fish pond or the girl from Bendigo Street.

When I heard the gospel I felt a heaviness pressing on me, but not for long. I was still only twelve years old, and the summer and the new church year were beginning. I had thought, as I thought every year on the last Sunday after Pentecost, of the end of the world drifting towards me like clouds or smoke from the direction of Europe or the Middle East; but then I had thought of a greenness within the greyness.

I was thinking every day of the settlement in the mountains between the King and the Broken. I was going to ask my parents not to take me to the other side of the city of Melbourne but to let me live with one of the families who grew potatoes in the red soil of clearings in the green forest and who sang the office of vespers and compline every evening in the timber chapel built with their own hands.

Something else kept me from feeling heaviness. Among the first words of the gospel for the last Sunday after Pentecost are the words addressed to the reader. I had always considered those words as addressed in a special sense to me.

Like many children, I was afraid of the end of the world. But even at the worst moment – even when the stars of heaven were falling and the sun was being darkened –

I could still hear the sound of the words being read. Not even the end of the world could drown out the sound of the words describing it.

I considered myself the Reader. Even after the greenness of the world had been buried under the greyness, the Reader would have to remain alive in order to read what the Writer had written about the green and the grey.

For twenty-five years, until I began to write on these pages, I would have said that the child had been right. I would have said that I had remained alive. I was alive and reading.

When I began to write on these pages I thought often about a person I called my reader. Sometimes I addressed the person named Reader. I could not think of words without a reader. I could not think of a reader who was not alive. But since I first began to write on these pages I have learned that a reader need not be alive. I can think of this page being read by a person who is dead as easily as you, reader, can think of this page as being written by someone who is dead.

Heaven and earth shall pass away but my words shall not pass away.

I had never expected my parents to allow me to travel to the mountains between the King River and the Broken River and to live there as I believed the Catholics of Europe had lived in the Middle Ages. I never actually saw the dark-green mountains with clearings of red soil

among the tall eucalypts and with long rows of green
potato-plants in the soil. Instead, I was taken just before
my thirteenth birthday to the district between Scotchman's
Creek and Elster Creek.

Before I left the old weatherboard house I scooped the
two goldfish out of the laundry trough in the backyard.
I carried the two fish to the other side of the city of
Melbourne in the same biscuit-tin that had carried them
from the fish pond behind the first house my parents had
owned to the house beside the sheep yards in the district
between the Ovens and Reedy Creek and then back to the
weatherboard house in my native district.

While I had been living in the weatherboard house,
the glass fish tank had been in storage with the rest of
my family's furniture. When the house was built in the
clearing among the tea-tree scrub, in the district between
Scotchman's Creek and Elster Creek, the furniture was
brought out from storage and my parents and my brothers
and I moved into the house. I set up the fish tank in the
fibro-cement shed behind the house. I spread pebbles
across the bottom of the tank, and I bought a few water
plants and pushed their roots in among the pebbles. But
I was no longer interested in the two fish. I only noticed the
fish when I sprinkled crumbs of fish food on the surface
of the tank every second afternoon. Occasionally on those
afternoons I saw a little raft of bubbles in a corner of
the tank or clinging to the floating leaf of a water plant.
I wondered whether the bubbles were eggs and whether,

if they were eggs, the fish might have been a male and a female after all. But the next day the bubbles would have gone. Either they had been mere bubbles and had burst or, if they were eggs, they had been eaten by the two fish.

One warm afternoon about a year after the fish had been taken from their brick pond, I went into the shed and saw one of the fish lying on the floor beside the tank. The fish was dead. Its scales were quite dry and the fins that had always looked transparent and soft in the water now looked whitish and were spiky to touch. I supposed the fish had thrown itself out of the water and over the shallow rim of the tank. I had sometimes seen fish flip themselves out of the water and then fall back again on hot evenings when I had sat on the edge of the brick pond a year or two earlier. I had thought that the leaps were connected with what I vaguely called breeding.

The fish in the shed had not fallen to the cement floor. I had laid flat on the floor beside the tank a plywood door left behind by the men who had built the house. I was using the rectangle of plywood as a base for a model railway layout. I had only a simple oval track but I was hoping to add loops and sidings. And already I had sketched on the wood beneath the layout of rails an approximate outline of part of the continent of North America; I was going to think of the wide landscapes of America while my engine and rolling-stock travelled around the circuit. The fish had flung itself from the fish tank almost to the centre of the rectangle of plywood.

The dying of that particular fish I always remembered afterwards. Of the other fish I remember nothing. I suppose I found it dead and floating in the tank one day. I can remember from the years after my first year in that house that the fish tank was sometimes filled with soil and that I tried to grow small flowering plants in the soil.

The cowherds pulled her out when they watered the cattle at dawn. By the time we arrived there on our way to school, she was lying on the thin ice formed by the water which had been spilt from the well. Under this covering the black clods of earth, the pieces of straw and dung glinted and sparkled like rare jewels under glass. There she lay with open eyes in which, like the small objects under the ice, was frozen the broken terror of a startled glance. Her mouth was open, her nose rather haughtily tilted, and on her forehead and beautiful cheeks there were huge scratches which had either occurred during her fall, or had been made by the cowherds as they let down the bucket before they caught sight of her among the ice-patches in the dark winter dawn. She was barefooted, she had left her boots in the assistant farm-manager's room, by the bed from which she had suddenly leapt and dashed straight as an arrow to the well.

I first read these words ten years ago, on a hot day in February. Early in the morning of that day I had closed the window of this room and had pulled down the blind in order to keep out the sunlight and the north wind. I had then taken a book down from one of the shelves and had sat at this table and begun to read.

The name of the book that I read on that hot day has

already been written on one of these pages. I had taken the book down from the shelf in the morning because I wanted to read a book about grasslands. Even then, ten years ago, I had grown tired of most of the books on my shelves. Each year I had read fewer books. The only books I was still interested in reading were books about grasslands.

Until that hot day in February I had never opened the covers of the book containing the words that I wrote on this page fifteen minutes ago. I took down the book from the shelf on that hot day because I understood that one of the words on the cover of the book was the word for *grassland* in the Magyar language.

Ten years ago I believed that any person named or referred to in a book was already dead. The person named on the cover of the book might have been alive or dead, but any person named or referred to inside the book was unquestionably dead.

On the hot day when I first read in a certain book the words beginning, *The cowherds pulled her out when they watered the cattle at dawn*...I did not at once cease to believe what I had believed all my life concerning the people named or referred to in books. What I did was to write on a page.

Of the many hundreds of pages I have written in this room, the first page I wrote was a letter. After I had written the letter I addressed it and posted it to a woman who had once lived in a street named Daphne in the district where I was born. Then I went on writing on other pages, every one of which is still lying somewhere around me in this room. On every day while I was writing on pages, I thought of the people referred to or named in the book with the word for *grassland* on its cover.

At first while I was writing I thought of those people as though they were all dead and I myself was alive. At some time while I was writing, however, I began to suspect what I am now sure of. I began to suspect that all persons named or referred to in the pages of books are alive, whereas all other persons are dead.

When I wrote the letter which was the first of all my pages, I was thinking of a young woman who was, I thought, dead while I was still alive. I thought the young woman was dead while I remained alive in order to go on writing what she could never read.

Today while I write on this last page, I am still thinking of the young woman. Today, however, I am sure the young woman is still alive. I am sure the young woman is still alive while I am dead. Today I am dead but the young woman remains alive in order to go on reading what I could never write.

Anyone standing at the corner of Landells Road and Sims Street, in the suburb of Pascoe Vale, would be one kilometre from the corner of a rectangle of about one and a half square kilometres of grass and scattered trees both native and European. The place of grass and trees is called Fawkner Crematorium and Memorial Park. A person standing at the corner of Landells Road and Sims Street today would see to the north-east only fences and gardens and windows and walls and roofs of houses built mostly in the last years of the 1950s. A person standing on the same corner in a year before any of those houses had been built would almost certainly have seen the tops of the trees in the Memorial Park but would probably not have seen any of the boundary fence of the Memorial

Park, so that the trees might have seemed merely a clump or a row of trees in the middle distance of a grassland.

Once each year, in the spring or the autumn, I travel by rail to Fawkner and then I walk for an hour through the grounds of the place that most people call simply Fawkner Cemetery.

If anyone asked me why I walk each year among the graves and the lawns and the patches of unkempt grass, I would answer that the cemetery is the only place I know where I can still see the plains to the north of Melbourne as they must have seemed before people from Europe arrived there. This would be a true answer, but in fact I have other reasons as well for visiting the cemetery.

I do not look directly at trees or grass while I walk in the cemetery. I aim my eyes ahead of me, but I notice only what lies to one or the other side of me. What I see in this way from the sides of my eyes is mostly more convincing, as though I had glimpsed what is present to the eyes of a person who keeps always to one side of me and a little behind me but whose judgement is much more sound and whose vision is much clearer than mine.

My second reason for visiting the cemetery at Fawkner is that I intend to have my body buried there. Each copy of my last will and testament has attached to it an instruction that my body may be either buried whole or burned first and buried afterwards, but that in either case my so-called remains must be put nowhere else than in the soil of my native district: the level and unremarkable land north of the city of Melbourne between the Moonee Ponds and the Merri creeks.

Like most people, I can only guess how much longer my body will last. But whether it lasts for thirty more years or only for the few days more that I need for writing on these pages, I am comfortable knowing that the end of my body will be the same in either case.

Like most people, I wonder sometimes about other places where I might have lived or gone on living if things had happened differently. I wonder sometimes about other memories of places and people that another man bearing my name might have called by now his life. And whenever I suppose that my body will last for many more years yet, I wonder about the different collections of items that might yet comprise what I will call after many more years my life. And during each of those many more years I may well wonder about other memories of places and people that one or another man bearing my name might have called by then his life.

Each year when I look around the cemetery at Fawkner I know I am looking at the place where all my lives, actual or conjectured, will end. Whoever I am, whoever I might otherwise have been, whoever I might yet become – the lives of all these men will end in the one grassland, only four kilometres from the street where I was born.

In the cemetery at Fawkner each year I look more often at grass and trees and birds than at graves. If I look at a grave I hardly expect to recognise the name on it. I know by name only one person whose grave is somewhere in the one and a half square kilometres of the Memorial Park. I have never seen that person's grave, and if ever I see the grave I will only have seen it by chance.

The person I am thinking of died between forty and fifty years ago. I know only his surname and that he was a small child when he died. I hardly ever think of the boy, but I remember each year when I walk in the cemetery that the grave of the boy is somewhere among the grass.

I know about the boy only that he lived a few years and then died, and I only know this because the sister of the boy mentioned him once to me when she and I were a girl and a boy each twelve years old. I had noticed that the girl seemed to have no sisters or brothers, and I asked her whether she was an only child. She then told me that she had once had a younger brother who had died when she herself was a small child, and that the grave of the boy was in Fawkner Cemetery.

I think often of the sister of the dead boy. I think of her always as a girl of twelve years or a year or two older, although by now, of course, the girl I knew in 1951 would be a woman as old as I am. I hardly ever think of the dead boy, except for a few minutes each year while I walk in the cemetery at Fawkner. Then I think that the boy's having died and been buried at Fawkner may have been the chief reason for his parents' having decided in 1950, in their rented cottage in the slums of East Melbourne, that of all the suburbs around Melbourne where brick veneer homes were being built and offered for sale they would choose to buy the first house they had bought in Pascoe Vale, where certain streets overlooked paddocks with a view of the distant trees in the cemetery at Fawkner.

Or I think that if the boy had not died when he died, then the girl I knew in 1951 would have had a younger brother. She might not have been the somewhat solitary girl who did not object to my talking to her sometimes, even though she risked being teased afterwards by some of her classmates. If the boy had not died, his sister might never have told me, as she once told me in 1951, that her only friend was the small dog that she hurried home to feed and to exercise each afternoon. If the boy had not died, the girl might never have owned the dog that barked on a few fine Sunday afternoons late in the winter and early in the spring of that year, causing the girl to look through the curtains of a front window and to see me loitering in the street with my own dog, having just come from Sims Street, where I had let my dog run loose while I stared to the north of me at the paddocks that I called my grasslands and at a line of trees that I did not then know were some of the trees of Fawkner Cemetery.

I think often of the girl whose brother died as a small child, but I could hardly suppose that the woman who was once the girl would think nowadays of me.

When I last saw that girl I was about to travel with my parents and brothers from my native district to a district two hundred kilometres away. I cannot remember talking to the girl or even seeing her in the last days that I spent in my native district. I have wanted for many years to remember that I felt during my last days in my native district something of the desolateness that I feel nowadays whenever I remember the house with the fish pond behind it and the girl who lived in Bendigo Street.

I remember mostly from my last days in Pascoe Vale that I looked often at a map of the district between the Ovens and Reedy Creek and that I urged my parents to buy a glass fish tank so that I could take two fish from the pond to the inland district. But I remember one thing else. I remember that the girl from Bendigo Street walked up to me on the first morning after I had spread the news at my school that I would soon be leaving the district. The girl asked me, as though it was a small matter to her, how far away was the district where I was going. I told her, as though it was a small matter to me, how far away was the district between the Ovens River and Reedy Creek. If the girl or I said anything to one another after that, I have not remembered it.

The girl had asked me her question as though it was a small matter to her, but I had read in her face that it was not a small matter to her, and I have not forgotten today what I read in her face.

I believe today that the girl from Bendigo Street would have thought of me often during the first weeks after I had left her district. She would have thought I was far inland in a district she had never seen. She could not have thought I was living in the parish of Saint Mark, Fawkner, only a half-hour's walk from Bendigo Street, and yet not thinking often of her.

If the woman who was once the girl from Bendigo Street has thought of me a few times since the year when I left her district, she has probably thought of me as still far inland and never thinking of her. She could hardly suppose that I think of her often and that I look out sometimes, in the cemetery at Fawkner, for the grave of her only brother, who died between forty and fifty years ago.

For most of my time in the cemetery I look at birds. I have never expected to see among the lawns and the plots of the cemetery the quail or the bustards or the almost-extinct species *Pedionomus torquatus*, the plains wanderer, that I sometimes dream about in dreams of grasslands. But one day in spring five years ago I saw a species I had never seen before in the cemetery or anywhere else.

The weather had been by turns sunny and cloudy. I was in the south-west corner of the cemetery. The sun began to shine. Then faint rain fell.

The rain was the same filmy rain that I think of whenever I read the last paragraph of the biography of Marcel Proust by André Maurois. When the mist of drops had passed over me I stood still and looked around as though I ought to have seen, after such rain, something unexpected.

I heard behind me tinkling calls of birds. A flock of small greyish birds was drifting through the tall stems of a patch of unmown grass. The drifting of the birds was like a further sprinkling of rain, but this time with flashes of yellow in the grey. I recognised the birds from colour-plates in books: the yellow-tailed thornbill, *Acanthiza chrysorrhoa*.

The stillness after the birds was even more noticeable than the earlier stillness after the rain, and I looked around again for a sign.

The only signs I am sure of are signs in words. In the cemetery after the birds had drifted past, I looked for the nearest words.

The nearest words were on the nearest grave. Some of the words were in English and some were in the Finnish language. In the grave was the body of a man who had been born in Tapiola twenty-seven years before I was born and who had died in my native district five years before I saw his grave.

I read the English words and the two dates on the grave of the Finn, and then I stared at some words in the Finnish language, which is incomprehensible to me.

While I stared I began to weep. I wept in a way that I have never wept for any person I have met during my life. I wept for only a few moments but violently, in the way that I weep sometimes for a man or a woman in a book that I have just read to its end.

I lingered round them, under that benign sky; watched the moths fluttering among the heath and hare-bells; listened to the soft wind breathing through the grass; and wondered how anyone could ever imagine unquiet slumbers, for the sleepers in that quiet earth.